# Adventures
## OF THE ELEMENTS

# Dangerous Games

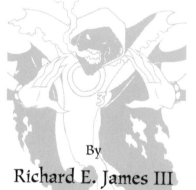

By

### Richard E. James III

Illustrations by Chad Welch

Edited by Maryann Lyle

www.AdventuresoftheElements.com

Library of Congress Control Number: 2004102820

ISBN: 0-9675901-2-4

Published by
Three Rivers Council #578, BSA for Learning for Life

Illustrated by
Chad Welch, www.cartoonimator.com

Editor
Maryann Lyle

From the developers of the Adventures of the Elements Trading Card Game, Three Rivers Council #578, comes the continuation of the *Adventures of the Elements* book series originated by Embassy Court Productions

www.adventuresoftheelements.com

Printed in the United States of America
Printing by Pine Hill Press, Inc.

This adventure is dedicated to my many friends without whose support the creation of the *Adventures of the Elements* would not have been possible. The value of genuine friendship is immeasurable, for it requires an unselfish and giving quality few ever truly realize. May we all be that altruistic friend to someone special in our lives. And may this act of "treating others the way we wish to be treated" pervade our daily lives in both family and in business relationships.

# PERIODIC TABLE

| 1<br>H<br>1.008 | | | | | | | | |
|---|---|---|---|---|---|---|---|---|
| 3<br>Li<br>6.941 | 4<br>Be<br>9.012 | | | | | | | |
| 11<br>Na<br>22.99 | 12<br>Mg<br>24.31 | | | | | | | |
| 19<br>K<br>39.10 | 20<br>Ca<br>40.08 | 21<br>Sc<br>44.96 | 22<br>Ti<br>47.87 | 23<br>V<br>50.94 | 24<br>Cr<br>52.00 | 25<br>Mn<br>54.94 | 26<br>Fe<br>55.85 | 27<br>Co<br>50.93 |
| 37<br>Rb<br>85.47 | 38<br>Sr<br>87.62 | 39<br>Y<br>88.91 | 40<br>Zr<br>91.22 | 41<br>Nb<br>92.91 | 42<br>Mo<br>95.94 | 43<br>Tc<br>(98) | 44<br>Ru<br>101.1 | 45<br>Rh<br>102.9 |
| 55<br>Cs<br>132.9 | 56<br>Ba<br>137.3 | 71<br>Lu<br>175.0 | 72<br>Hf<br>178.5 | 73<br>Ta<br>180.9 | 74<br>W<br>183.8 | 75<br>Re<br>186.2 | 76<br>Os<br>190.2 | 77<br>Ir<br>192.2 |
| 87<br>Fr<br>(223) | 88<br>Ra<br>(226) | 103<br>Lr<br>(262) | 104<br>Rf<br>(261) | 105<br>Db<br>(262) | 106<br>Sg<br>(266) | 107<br>Bh<br>(264) | 108<br>Hs<br>(269) | 109<br>Mt<br>(268) |

| 57<br>La<br>138.9 | 58<br>Ce<br>140.1 | 59<br>Pr<br>140.9 | 60<br>Nd<br>144.2 | 61<br>Pm<br>(145) |
|---|---|---|---|---|
| 89<br>Ac<br>(227) | 90<br>Th<br>232.0 | 91<br>Pa<br>231.0 | 92<br>U<br>238.0 | 93<br>Np<br>(237) |

|  |  |  |  |  |  |  |  | 2<br>He<br>4.003 |
|---|---|---|---|---|---|---|---|---|
|  |  | 5<br>B<br>10.81 | 6<br>C<br>12.01 | 7<br>N<br>14.01 | 8<br>O<br>16.00 | 9<br>F<br>19.00 | 10<br>Ne<br>20.18 |  |
|  |  | 13<br>Al<br>26.98 | 14<br>Si<br>28.09 | 15<br>P<br>30.97 | 16<br>S<br>32.06 | 17<br>Cl<br>35.45 | 18<br>Ar<br>39.95 |  |

Ca 20

| 28<br>Ni<br>58.69 | 29<br>Cu<br>63.55 | 30<br>Zn<br>65.41 | 31<br>Ga<br>69.72 | 32<br>Ge<br>72.64 | 33<br>As<br>74.92 | 34<br>Se<br>78.96 | 35<br>Br<br>79.90 | 36<br>Kr<br>83.80 |
|---|---|---|---|---|---|---|---|---|
| 46<br>Pd<br>106.4 | 47<br>Ag<br>107.9 | 48<br>Cd<br>112.4 | 49<br>In<br>114.8 | 50<br>Sn<br>118.7 | 51<br>Sb<br>121.8 | 52<br>Te<br>127.6 | 53<br>I<br>126.9 | 54<br>Xe<br>131.3 |
| 78<br>Pt<br>195.1 | 79<br>Au<br>197.0 | 80<br>Hg<br>200.6 | 81<br>Tl<br>204.4 | 82<br>Pb<br>207.2 | 83<br>Bi<br>209.0 | 84<br>Po<br>(209) | 85<br>At<br>(210) | 86<br>Rn<br>(222) |
| 110<br>Ds<br>(271) | 111<br>Uuu<br>(272) | 112<br>Uub<br>(285) | 113<br>Uut | 114<br>Uuq<br>(289) | 115<br>Uup | 116<br>Uuh<br>(292) | 117<br>Uus | 118<br>Uuo<br>(?) |

| 62<br>Sm<br>150.4 | 63<br>Eu<br>152.0 | 64<br>Gd<br>157.3 | 65<br>Tb<br>158.9 | 66<br>Dy<br>162.5 | 67<br>Ho<br>164.9 | 68<br>Er<br>167.3 | 69<br>Tm<br>168.9 | 70<br>Yb<br>173.0 |
|---|---|---|---|---|---|---|---|---|
| 94<br>Pu<br>(244) | 95<br>Am<br>(243) | 96<br>Cm<br>(247) | 97<br>Bk<br>(247) | 98<br>Cf<br>(251) | 99<br>Es<br>(252) | 100<br>Fm<br>(257) | 101<br>Md<br>(258) | 102<br>No<br>(259) |

O 8

P 15

K

Ta 73

Xe 54

## CHAPTER ONE
### Episode Nine
# "Field of Screams"

Cold, dark eyes bore into his skull. Planting both feet firmly in the closely cropped, sun-scorched grass, he stared at the mammoth onrushing figure. Fear and awe clouded his mind. There remained time to avoid the imminent collision, but his pride refused to allow him to budge. With his lungs laboring for air, the young lad's chest rose and fell beneath his protective covering. Perspiration beaded on his brow and rolled into his eyes, causing him to grimace in pain. Richard fought to push the agony that ripped through his side from his mind. Despite his dismal condition, Richard supposed he would survive long enough to be crushed and buried by his opponent.

Deliberately, the charging bullish form lowered his head. The sun glinted off the combatant's helmet. Richard closed his eyes and tightly clenched his teeth awaiting the inevitable bone-crunching impact. For a moment time froze. Then the silence was shattered, ruptured by the ear-splitting crash of one warrior slamming into another.

Landing with a thud, Richard stared into the blue sky, struggling to breathe in the thick humid air. His opponent, stumbling over Richard's motionless body, fell forward onto the hard field. In disgust the massive gladiator scrambled to his feet and stood over his fallen victim. Three more armor-clad giants encircled the dazed fifteen-year-old.

"Are you okay? Oh, man, what a hit! You saved the touchdown," shouted one of the players, removing his football helmet.

"I did? I saved the touchdown? I can't believe it," mumbled Richard, staggering to his feet with the aid of his teammates and coach.

"It looks like you'll be okay, sport. You got your bell rung, but you'll shake it off. Great hit!" said the coach, placing Richard's arm around his shoulder to prevent the dizzy youth from collapsing. "How many fingers do you see, Son?"

Shaking his head and unbuckling his chinstrap, Richard squinted and stared at the coach's hand, "Three?"

"Close enough, I'll guide you to the sidelines. You may feel slightly woozy, but it won't last long."

"That's the way I want to see you guys hit! That's what I've been talking about all summer. Let's put some fear into the other team. We won't be intimidated by anybody!" yelled a tall man, clapping from the side of the field.

"Thanks, Coach, but I don't think I scared him. He ran over me."

"That may be true, but you don't let him think that," assured the coach, his mouth partially concealed beneath a bushy black mustache. "He may have gotten up faster, but he felt the blow. He'll have his share of bruises in the morning. Next time, he won't be so aggressive when running through the line. That's all we need to force a fumble. You made him question how tough he is. And believe me, he doesn't think he's all that tough at the moment. Hang in there, kid. It's all in the mind."

*If it's all in the mind, then why do my ribs feel like someone pounded me with a sledgehammer?* thought Richard limping along the sidelines toward the aluminum benches. *It's easy for coach to tell us to suck it up and be tough. He's not the one out there getting clobbered. Ouch, my head won't quit ringing.*

"Sit here for a minute, and you'll be ready to go once our offense takes a crack at it. I'll have someone grab you a water bottle."

"Why didn't you use your ring?" asked Richard's younger brother, plopping onto the bench next to him.

"Anthony, you know the elements' rules. We can't use the rings unless it's a life or death situation and then only three times a day. Besides, I taped over it so coach wouldn't know I was wearing it on the football field. You know how he hates for us to wear jewelry in a game."

"I know, but Bro', that was a life or death situation. I thought we were going to have your funeral out there."

"Not today," answered Richard, elbowing his brother. "Hey, let's put on our element glasses."

"That hit must have knocked your brains out. Coach will kill us if he catches us wearing sunglasses. I don't want to run up and down the bleachers all afternoon."

"You are such a scout! Live on the edge a little. What if some evil molecule is watching us? I'd hate for Urban Carbon Monoxide to be sneaking through the field in front of us. Or even worse, what if our three little sisters accidentally got trapped in ancient Greece again? Only the element guardians would know, and they wouldn't be able to tell us because we aren't wearing our element glasses."

Sighing, Anthony reached for his glasses protruding from the top of his duffel bag. "If we get caught, I'm blaming it all on you."

"On me?" asked Ned Nitrogen, pointing innocently at himself. The little element guardian winked at the brothers. His blue cape fluttered in the gentle breeze. A thin smile crossed his wide face. Rubbing his large chin, Ned Nitrogen maneuvered his slender body through the air with ease. The circular clasp for his cape prominently displayed the letter "N."

"No, not you," answered Anthony, quickly scanning the football field and the surrounding bleachers. Catching a glimpse of a pale blue shape oozing under the opposing team's bench, Anthony bolted from his seat. "What is that?"

"What?"

"That blue thing under the bench across the field, what is it?" Anthony asked, pointing and stepping onto the field to more closely observe the mysterious object.

Hysterically waving his arms, Richard shouted, "Anthony, watch out!"

"Get off the field!" yelled the coach, galloping along the sidelines and wildly waving his clipboard. His overhanging belly shook with each stride.

"Wha...what?" stammered Anthony, watching the pale blue creature rise above the bench flashing a wicked grin.

A sparkling "$O_3$" radiated from beneath the strange being's ragged, frayed cloak. Keeping his head slightly bent, the creature managed to conceal the rest of his facial features under the dark shadow cast by the cloak's hood. Its massive form grew larger, dwarfing the opposing team's players who intently watched the game unaware of the ominous presence.

"Anthony!" hollered Richard.

Distracted by Richard's outcry, Anthony spun around to stare into a large, silver "eighty-two" before being knocked off his feet by the onrushing wide receiver. The crushing impact leveled the unsuspecting number eighty-two and tripped the defending cornerback, slamming him into the cracking, sun-baked field. The football landed with a thud and bounced out of bounds, rolling to a stop at the coach's

4

feet. Shrill whistles sounded, penalty flags landed around Anthony, football helmets flew, the coach's clipboard soared through the air, and three players sprawled motionless upon the ground. The coach's face turned three shades of red. Mumbling under his breath, he kicked the football down the sidelines and stomped onto the field.

Arriving at the crash site first, Richard quickly scooped up Anthony's element glasses and hid them under his jersey. "Is everybody alive?"

"I hope so," groaned Anthony, holding his head and pulling himself into a seated position. "I never saw him coming."

"I know. Arvis can you hear me?" asked Richard, placing a hand on number eighty-two's shoulder.

"Yeah, tell your brother to save a tackle like that for the game. But use it on the other team. I need to catch my breath," responded Arvis, inhaling and exhaling in wheezing gasps.

Towering over Anthony, the coach demanded an explanation, "What was going through your head kid? You're lucky you have a head after a collision like that."

"Coach, you need to get your player off the field," ordered the referee, picking up one of the yellow flags. "And I'm assessing both a personal foul and a penalty for too many men on the field. We're lucky no one was injured." Shaking his head, the referee directed his attention to the numerous players from both teams clustered around the accident scene. "Everybody back to the sidelines. No one's hurt. Let's play ball."

"Your brother is in serious trouble now," whispered Arvis, buckling his chinstrap and jogging to the huddle.

"Anthony, I want to see you running, not jogging, up and down those bleachers for the rest of this scrimmage," ordered the coach, pointing to the empty stadium.

"But coach, I didn't mean to hit..."

"I don't want to hear it. That's not the way a Jaguar plays this game. Why are you still standing here? Move it!"

"Yes, sir," said Anthony, trotting off the field. Passing Richard, who sprinted to match his brother's pace, Anthony inquired about his missing glasses.

"I've got your glasses. Ouch, slow down. Even though my head feels better, my leg hurts from that hit earlier. What were you doing?"

"We can't slow down. There's a monster creeping around on the other side of the field. Give me my glasses and get yours. I'll show you."

"I've got mine right here. For your sake, I hope there's something over there."

Handing Anthony the red pair of element glasses, Richard secured his glasses across the bridge of his nose. Leaping the first series of steps, Anthony reluctantly latched the frames of his glasses behind his ears and came to an abrupt halt. Richard immediately crashed into the back of his brother. Stumbling over one another and collapsing in a pile on the bleachers, the two boys stared in horror and attempted to suppress the screams rising in their throats.

"Looking for me?" inquired the looming $O_3$ creature. Green toxic gas escaped through the gaps in his badly decayed teeth. Rotten flesh hung from his scarred and wrinkled face.

# CHAPTER TWO
## Episode Ten
# "Pool of Fear"

"Adrienne, I'll get you!" yelled Jacqueline, swinging a Styrofoam pool noodle like a mighty club and charging through the chlorinated water. The deep blue pool welcomed the children's gleeful squeals and shouts. Even the unbearable temperature and the sun's scorching rays failed to divert the girl's attention from their play. The refreshing pool vanquished all thoughts of the intense afternoon heat.

"Jacqueline, don't make me splash you again," said Adrienne, backing away from Jacqueline and her noodle.

"Get her!" squealed Jeanne-Marie, grabbing Daina's arm and dragging her into the middle of Jacqueline and her friend's comical struggle for pool dominance.

Catherine and her companion, Tiffany, rested on the pool's outer edge watching the younger girls' commotion. All three sisters, Catherine, Jacqueline, and Jeanne-Marie, wore their element glasses without their friends realizing the glasses were anything more than ordinary sunglasses. Although they were strange looking sunglasses, none of the girls had questioned the three sisters about them. Smiling, Catherine winked at Caspar Calcium lazily floating at the opposite end of the pool from the thrashing, boisterous girls.

"I love Fridays," Tiffany proclaimed, adjusting the strap of her polka-dot swimsuit. "Too bad your brothers have to miss out on all of the fun. But I guess they like playing football, too."

"Yeah, it makes them feel macho. Then they come home and whine about their injuries," responded Catherine, sweep-

7

ing her hands back and forth in wide, gentle arcs across the water's surface.

"Whoa, Catherine, stop," ordered Caspar Calcium, shaking his silvery-white fist at the giggling girl. "You're making too many waves and soaking my chalk tooth necklace. Chalk and water are not a good combination."

"Oops, sorry," said Catherine, placing her hands on top of her head.

"What did you say?" asked Tiffany, staring at Catherine through narrowed, confused eyes.

"Oh, nothing."

"Don't start that again. Are you okay? Ever since you had to write all those lines in class, you've been saying weird stuff. Are you seeing ghosts or hearing voices?"

"Um, no, I...I'm okay. I just thought I had stepped on your foot. Forget about class. That was a weird day. I don't expect anything like that to happen again," answered Catherine, recalling her first encounter with the element guardian Caspar Calcium and the evil molecule Litharge Lead Monoxide.

Unfortunately, that day had caused her more trouble than she wished to remember. At least Litharge was now locked in Molecule Prison. She hoped he would stay there forever.

"Hey, I'm about to grab something to eat. It looks like Jacqueline is already wolfing down another hot dog. She must have escaped Adrienne and her noodle. I better get something before it's all gone," said Tiffany, climbing out of the pool and grabbing an oversized beach towel.

"Okay, I'll be there in a minute."

Watching Tiffany amble over to the grill sizzling with hot dogs, links, and hamburgers, Catherine, for a moment, wished she was free of the responsibility of being a human guardian. *But then who would protect my family and friends from the dangerous molecules lurking in the shadows?* she thought. *Besides, if I hadn't met the element guardians, I wouldn't have my element glasses or my ring with the emerald stone, which gives me the power of the element beryllium. Without this power I wouldn't be able to use my X-ray vision. If I didn't have my powers, then neither would my sisters and brothers have their rings and abilities. We'd be missing out on an awesome experience.* Drifting toward the center of the pool, Catherine slowly approached Caspar Calcium cautiously avoiding creating waves.

"Catherine, you're blocking my sunlight," groaned Caspar Calcium, paddling feverishly with his hands in an attempt to escape Catherine's shadow.

Laughing, Ollie Oxygen floated over the neighbor's wooden, picket fence and hovered above Catherine. "You two are always bumping heads and getting each other into precarious predicaments. By the way, Caspar Calcium, you'll never get a golden tan like Augustus Aurium. He's the only gold element. Although there are bronze alloys but those are made up of twenty percent tin and eighty percent copper. Too bad there is no calcium involved in making bronze. You will have to stay the same color."

"I know. But, the sun makes me shinier and brighter. Hey, did you check on Richard and Anthony."

"No, Ned Nitrogen is with them and Xerxes Xenon is on his way even though he believes football is too barbaric and primitive for the noble class. It reminds him of the days of the Romans and their gladiator tournaments."

"That sounds like him..."

"Cannonball!" screamed Jacqueline and Adrienne in unison.

Both girls leapt from the poolside clasping their legs tightly against their bodies and plunged into the water drenching Catherine and the invisible Caspar Calcium. Jeanne-Marie and Daina followed the two older girls' lead by diving into the pool and pummeling Catherine with long Styrofoam noodles. Catherine flailed her arms to no avail.

"That does it!" yelled Catherine, ripping a noodle from Jeanne-Marie's hand and playfully beating the four retreating girls on the head.

Caspar Calcium slowly paddled his way to the side and climbed out of the pool. Dripping wet, he glared at Jacqueline who couldn't quit laughing and who had to eventually clamber out of the pool to catch her breath and to regain her composure. Drying himself with the edge of Adrienne's towel hanging from one of the plastic chairs lining the pool, Caspar Calcium flopped on the concrete and closed his eyes. He draped a muscular arm over his face to block the sun's rays. His spear, planted in the ground near the concrete's edge, swayed in the breeze.

"You look like a fish out of water," said Ollie Oxygen, laughing and reclining on the arm of one of the chairs. Caspar Calcium pretended not to hear Ollie Oxygen's remark. Smiling and closing his eyes, Ollie Oxygen sighed deeply. Both elements quickly slipped into a tranquil slumber.

Standing alone in the center of the pool, Catherine waved her toy noodle victoriously in the air. "I am master of the pool! No one can beat me!"

"Has anyone seen Adrienne?" asked Jacqueline, scanning the pool.

"Maybe she went in the house," suggested Daina, sitting on the edge of the pool.

"No, she was right over there. I just saw..."

"Oh my...wha...what..." stammered Catherine, staring at the deep end of the pool.

A yellow-green gas rose from the water's surface. Below the surface, Adrienne floated face down in the pool. A strong, suffocating odor wafted over the girls irritating their eyes and throats.

Coughing violently, Jacqueline pointed at Adreinne's limp body. "Somebody help me. Adrienne's drowning!"

"Adrienne!" screamed Jeanne-Marie, frantically climbing out of the pool and running to the house. "Mamma, help. Adrienne's drowning."

Jeanne-Marie's mother raced out of the house to witness Catherine, Jacqueline, Tiffany, and Daina dragging Adrienne into the shade cast by a large elm tree near the pool. The girls were relieved to see Adrienne's chest rise and fall as she sucked in the warm, humid air. The yellow-green gas continued rising from the pool until it blanketed both the pool and the surrounding patio.

"I think she'll be okay," said Tiffany, kneeling over Adrienne and brushing her wet hair from her face. "But I don't feel good. I...I feel dizzy. The ground is spinning. I'm going to pass..." stammered Tiffany, collapsing on the patio.

"Tiffany!" shouted Catherine, kneeling over her friend and gently lifting her head.

"I don't feel good either," complained Daina, grabbing her stomach and sitting cross-legged on the patio. "My throat burns. My head..." sputtered Daina, slumping unconscious on the ground.

"What's happening to everyone?" asked Jeanne-Marie, a tear trickling down her cheek.

"I don't know," answered the three sisters' mother racing toward the back door. "It might be food poisoning. Wait there. I'm calling nine-one-one."

"It's not food poisoning. It's the pool," noted Catherine, standing and staring at the swirling yellow-green haze. In disbelief, Catherine and her two sisters watched the spiraling, rising gas.

"It's not the pool," seethed a voice from within the noxious gas. Two fiery eyes and a blinding "$Cl_2$" flickered from the fumes' murky depths.

# "Game Over"

"Run!" screamed Ned Nitrogen. "I'll try to slow him down. By the power of the elements, I summon nitrogen!"

A dazzling liquid nitrogen stream shot from Ned Nitrogen's clenched fist slamming into the $O_3$ creature. Unfazed by the miniature element's blast, the decaying fiend casually swept the frozen nitrogen patch from his cloak. Turning his attention from the boys, he glared at Ned Nitrogen through piercing, dagger-like eyes glowing from under his cloak's hood. Snorting, the monstrosity expelled suffocating, green vapor.

"I'm not here to toy with you, Ned Nitrogen. Leave while you still have the chance, or you will incur my wrath. I came to destroy the human race beginning with these human guardians. Their rings are useless against me!" snarled the hideous figure, pointing a gnarled finger at the brothers.

Struggling to their feet, the two boys sprinted along the lower level of the stadium. Richard no longer felt the pain in his side or leg. Fear clouded his thoughts. The monster's threats rang in his ears.

"We're dead!" blurted Anthony, racing after his brother.

Glancing at the bleachers, the coach spun around, astonished by the two boys sprinting along the stadium. "I must have been too rough on the kid. Maybe it was only an accident," mumbled the coach, scratching his head. "Hey, Arvis."

"Yes, Coach."

"Go get those two out of the stands and tell them to come see me."

13

"Yes, sir," answered Arvis, cutting across the sidelines in an attempt to intercept the two brothers. "Hey, Anthony, you can stop running. Richard, Anthony, Coach said to go see him. Can you hear me? I said you can stop."

"Arvis, get out of here," yelled Richard, streaking past his bewildered friend. Looking over his shoulder, Richard's eyes grew wide with fear. "Arvis, run!"

The wicked, cloaked figure extended his palm toward Ned Nitrogen emitting a pale-bluegreen-streaked gas. The toxic fumes choked the element guardian. Grabbing his throat, Ned Nitrogen coughed violently. His body fell limp and he tumbled to the earth. Matter-of-factly turning his head to confront the boys, the sinister being raised his arms and swooped down from the stadium steps. Drifting inches above the ground, the $O_3$ wretch gained on the brothers with every stride they made.

"He's going to catch us!" screamed Anthony, surging past Arvis on the heels of his brother.

"Who's going to catch you? I'm not. If you want to run all day, that's your business. You can have it," said Arvis, waving his hands demonstratively with each word he spoke. "What's wrong with you two? Coach said you can stop. Where are you going? That's the football field. Don't go out there again."

"He got Ned Nitrogen. We're dead! We're dead!" panted Richard, hurdling the team's bench.

"Look, there's Xerxes Xenon," shouted Anthony, crossing onto the playing field and pointing at a noble element with a large "Xe" imprinted on his torso and a jeweled crown on his head.

"This way. Follow me into that thicket of Loblolly pines!" shouted Xerxes Xenon, motioning to the boys from across the field.

14

"Where are they going? Are they crazy? Stop!" yelled the coach, slamming his clipboard against his thigh. "Get off the field. Did you get your brains knocked out in that collision earlier? Richard, where are you going? Is this an inherited family trait?"

The coach clutched his forehead and clenched his teeth. Players shrugged their shoulders in confusion. Whistles sounded and yellow flags flew.

"Coach Lee, if you can't control your boys, you will be required to forfeit the scrimmage," yelled the referee, scooping his flag off the ground.

"I'll control them. They're both off the team. How's that?" asked Coach Lee, slapping his baseball cap against his polyester coaching pants. "Did you two hear me?" he yelled. "You're suspended from the team."

"Suspended, who cares? We're dead," whimpered Anthony, scaling a wire fence and following his brother and Xerxes Xenon into the spruce grove.

"Stop here," said Xerxes Xenon, hovering above the two brothers.

Bending at the waist and supporting themselves with their hands clutching the knees of their football pants, the two boys gasped for breath. Watching the looming figure draw closer, Richard and Anthony scooted deeper into the tree cluster. Richard shuffled his feet to get into position to begin running again when the creature halted at the tree line.

"Why'd he stop?" asked Richard, straightening himself.

"Trees absorb ozone during photosynthesis. $O_3$ is the chemical symbol for the molecule ozone. You are staring at Ozzie Ozone, a stronger pollutant than carbon monoxide," said Xerxes Xenon, adjusting his cape.

"Oh great, we're definitely dead!" moaned Anthony, remembering their life-threatening encounter with the villainous Urban Carbon Monoxide.

"Very clever, Xerxes Xenon, but they can't stay in the woods forever. I can wait," growled Ozzie Ozone, releasing bursts of toxic gas from under his hooded cloak. "In the meantime let's see how those puny humans in the field can handle one of my potions. A touch of ozone and a few existing pollutants mixed with the sunlight creates an intoxicating concoction, a brew that you call smog, more specifically referred to as photochemical smog."

Before the brothers or Xerxes Xenon could react, Ozzie Ozone turned and raised both hands skyward, pointing his fingers in the direction of the football field. Electric sparks erupted from his fingertips. Pale-blue and green streaks burst into the air. Spiraling like a tornado, the gaseous stripes materialized into rolling gray smog that rapidly blanketed the field, players, coaches, and referees.

"What's going on?" asked Coach Lee, rolling his eyes and staring toward the heavens. "Where is this smog coming from? What else could possibly go wrong today?"

"I can't see my hand in front of my face," said Arvis, coughing violently. "My eyes burn. I'm getting out of here!"

"The game is over. Scrimmage is canceled," yelled one of the referees, choking in the thick smog.

Panic gripped the players scrambling frantically around the field. Unable to see, several players succumbed to the sickening smog. Screams of terror filled the stadium. Players, coaches, and referees collapsed on the field. Desperate cries for help were quickly swallowed by the toxic fumes.

"No one will escape," cackled Ozzie Ozone, releasing a hideous, guttural, hissing laugh. "You Homo sapiens think you are an intelligent, superior species. What a farce. I've seen more astute mice! What else could possibly go wrong today?" he mocked. "How about your funeral?"

# "Clifton Chlorine"

"Caspar Calcium, Ollie Oxygen, help!" screamed Jeanne-Marie, staring with wide, saucer-shaped eyes into the flaming jewels flickering from within the suffocating gas.

"What's wrong?" asked Ollie Oxygen, snapping out of his peaceful snooze.

"Oh, no," muttered Caspar Calcium, sitting upright and surveying the chaotic scene before him.

"My eyes burn!" cried Jeanne-Marie, removing her glasses with a trembling hand and rubbing her eyelids. "My throat hurts. I can't breathe!"

"Tell Jeanne-Marie to put on her glasses. If she removes her element glasses, she'll end up like the others. The glasses will help to protect you as long as you don't get too close to Clifton Chlorine."

"Jeanne-Marie, put on your glasses. They'll make you feel better," instructed Catherine.

"Clifton Chlorine, is he an element?" asked Jacqueline, retreating from the pool, but not before managing to cast a menacing scowl at the gaseous figure. "Why is he trying to hurt us?"

"Yes," hissed the voice from the pool. "I am chlorine..."

"I don't care who you are. What did you do to my friends?" No longer backing away, Jacqueline planted herself squarely before the ominous element. Thrusting her shoulders back, the young strawberry-blond tightly clenched her fists. Pausing, she lowered her head and looked at her fists. Her golden ring with the purple amethyst stone flashed in the bright sunlight. Jerking her head up, Jacqueline jabbed her clenched right hand at the gaseous element.

Catherine and Jeanne-Marie stood rigidly, gaping open-mouthed at the confrontation between their sister and Clifton Chlorine. The searing heat caused beads of perspiration to trickle down Catherine's forehead and into her eyes. Yet she dared not remove her glasses to rub her eyes for fear of succumbing to the toxic chlorine gas.

Glowering at the heinous element, Jacqueline held her ring aloft, "By the power of the alkaline earth metals, I summon magnesium!"

"What? How?" stammered Clifton Chlorine, unable to avoid the dazzling purple blast from Jacqueline's ring.

Jacqueline's purple stream encircled Clifton Chlorine's vaporous figure. The element's burning eyes flashed and then faded to a dull yellow hue. Stunned, the chlorine element hovered silently above the pool offering no resistance against Jacqueline's attack. Gradually, the little "two" on the $Cl_2$ in the center of the gas vanished. In a blinding flash, a small yellow element with a yellow-green cape and a "Cl" on his torso splashed into the pool amidst a flurry of silver-white salt.

"What...What happened?" asked Catherine, grabbing Jacqueline and pulling her from the edge of the pool. "Where did he go? I don't see him."

"I can't find him either," answered Ollie Oxygen, scanning the mounds of salt piled around the pool. "I think you shocked him with your ring. He didn't know the Great Ones had given each of you the power of one of the element guardians through your Rings of Enlightenment."

"I could see the shock in his eyes," said Caspar Calcium, peering into the pool. "Your magnesium combined with his chlorine to create a salt called magnesium chloride. That is one effective way to eliminate some forms of pollution. Too bad we can't borrow a wet-gas scrubber from one of the refineries. That would eliminate chlorine gas completely."

"What happened to the little "two" next to his "Cl?"" asked Jacqueline, huddling next to her sisters.

"Oh, Clifton Chlorine, like Io Iodine, is from the mystical family of the Halogens. He, like Io Iodine, has the power to create a magical diatomic molecule by connecting to another identical chlorine atom to form chlorine gas."

"Is he more powerful than the other element guardians?"

"No, but Clifton Chlorine's strength lies in his ability to combine easily with other elements to create many different molecules. Fortunately, this is also a weakness since we can sometimes force him to create relatively harmless compounds like magnesium chloride."

"You are the weak ones!" snarled Clifton Chlorine, squatting behind a radio blaring rhythmic tunes from a table near the pool. "I will not be so easily taken by your rings this time."

Before the other elements could react, Clifton Chlorine gave a great heave and shoved the radio into the pool. Sparks leapt about the water's surface. Showing no fear of the electrically charged pool, Clifton Chlorine dove into the water following the radio's path.

"No!" screamed Ollie Oxygen. "Get away from the pool!"

With the music silenced beneath the water, the yard grew hauntingly quiet. As if blown by a gentle breeze, the tops of the salt mounds swirled even though the humid, stale air failed to move. Again the magnesium chloride salt shifted position. With a flash, the salt swirled violently about the pool and exploded into a yellow-green gas. Small pieces of silver-white magnesium metal showered the pool and surrounding patio.

Laughing hideously, Clifton Chlorine materialized in the middle of the gas with a large "$Cl_2$" in the middle of his figure. Peering through two cutting eyes, he challenged the children and elements, "Try those rings again. I dare you. I have no time to play trivial games with you. There is your magnesium metal scattered around the pool. You fools! You should have known magnesium chloride can be separated into magnesium and chlorine gas by passing an electric current through it. That's electrolysis at work. I guess your friends, the so-called element guardians, forgot to tell you or maybe they don't know as much as they think they know. Oh well, it doesn't matter. Your time has come. Face the wrath of chlorine!"

"Not so fast!" yelled Ollie Oxygen, springing into the air and hovering over the barbecue pit. "By the power of the nonmetallic elements, I summon oxygen!" Blue air currents blasted from his clenched fists, momentarily dispersing the thick chlorine gas making it easier for the girls to breathe.

"Very clever, Ollie Oxygen. But I won't let you stop my suffocating gas by blowing oxygen through it. You can't make enough oxygen to thin my poisonous cloud. The girls are doomed, and so are you," snarled Clifton Chlorine, pointing a gaseous hand at the oxygen element.

"Ollie Oxygen, get away from the grill!" screamed Caspar Calcium, running to the pool's edge as fast as his short, stout legs could carry him.

Before Ollie Oxygen could react to Caspar Calcium's warning, Clifton Chlorine sprayed the smoldering coals with chlorine. A violent explosion slammed Ollie Oxygen into the brick patio, scattering hamburger patties and hot dogs across the yard. Releasing a ghastly cackle, Clifton Chlorine contentedly observed Ollie Oxygen's motionless form.

"No..." Trembling with rage, Caspar Calcium jerked his spear from the ground and flung it into the gas. The spear disappeared into the mist. Extending his outstretched fingers toward the chlorine cloud, Caspar Calcium chanted, "By the power of the alkaline-earth metals, I summon calcium!"

A shower of white, chalk-like flakes rained upon the chlorine cloud. Desperately, Clifton Chlorine attempted to retaliate with a toxic blast. Shifting his gaseous cloud like a rapidly rolling fog, he backed away from the chalk flurry. But it was too late, Clifton Chlorine's deadly blast fizzled to a thin haze and his eyes dulled to yellow. Once again the "$Cl_2$" on his torso wavered for a moment before being replaced with a "Cl." Raising two tiny clenched fists skyward, Clifton Chlorine released a guttural scream and splashed into the pool amidst a shower of salt.

"He won't reappear for now. He is too weak to make another cloud. He probably combined with the water to create dilute hydrochloric acid. The rest of him combined with my calcium to produce calcium chloride. The only thing that molecule is useful for is melting ice on streets and reducing dust."

"Good riddance," mumbled Jacqueline, glaring at the spot in the pool where Clifton Chlorine disappeared.

"I hear sirens..."

"Girls, the ambulance is on the way. Everything will be okay," assured the girls' mother, racing out of the house and opening the gate leading to the driveway.

"Oh, my head," groaned Ollie Oxygen, propping himself into a seated position.

"It's a good thing you wore your helmet. Otherwise a hit like that might have seriously injured you," said Caspar Calcium, retrieving his spear from where it had wedged itself in the stump of a rose bush.

"Here they come!" yelled the girls' mother, waving frantically from the driveway.

Shouting over screeching tires and the siren's deafening, high-pitched wail, Caspar Calcium directed the girls, "Tell the emergency crew you think your friends are suffering from inhaling chlorine gas. They'll know what to do."

The yard flooded with blue-uniformed paramedics, stretchers, and medical equipment. The girls' mother nervously held her head in her hands. Catherine, Jacqueline, and Jeanne-Marie were quickly ushered into the ambulance for testing and for further observation for any signs of chlorine gas poisoning.

CHAPTER FIVE
Episode Nine

# "Smog"

"We've got to help them," said Anthony, regaining his breath and confidence as the tree canopy prevented Ozzie Ozone from advancing any further.

"I'll help them!" hissed Ozzie Ozone, flashing a rotten-toothed grin at the two brothers and Xerxes Xenon. "In fact, I think I'll take a closer look at our hapless victims. I'm sure their faces should be contorted into gruesomely beautiful expressions by this point. Don't try to run away. I'll be back."

Fuming with rage at Ozzie Ozone's devilish laughter and brazen demeanor, Anthony clenched his fists, and, through narrowed eyes, watched the molecule glide toward the playing field. After a moment, he disappeared into the thick smog. The two brothers turned to Xerxes Xenon with blank expressions, exhausted by the day's events and their apparently hopeless predicament.

"Quickly, Richard, use your ring. Make a large mirror and aim it at the smog. Hurry before that fiend, Ozzie Ozone, returns," urged Xerxes Xenon, anxiously scanning the smog-covered field.

Scratching his head, Richard peered quizzically at Xerxes Xenon and shrugged his shoulders. "I don't get it. Are we trying to scare him with his reflection? I know he's one ugly monster but..."

"Do I have to explain everything? If everyone had the fine breeding of the noble gases, we would not have to waste our time explaining such trivial matters. What manner of universities do you simpletons attend?" grumbled Xerxes Xenon, massaging his forehead with his fingertips. "Oh, never mind, as you should know, ozone can do good as well as evil. In fact, ozone creates the ozone layer, which protects the earth from the sun's damaging ultraviolet rays. To put it simply, ozone protects us by absorbing the ultraviolet light. When the ozone, with the symbol "$O_3$," absorbs these rays, it decomposes or breaks into an oxygen element, with the symbol "O," and an oxygen molecule, with the chemical symbol "$O_2$.""

"Wow, so Ozzie Ozone will break apart if we hit him with enough of the sun's ultraviolet light," blurted Anthony, wringing his hands excitedly.

"Basically, yes," said Xerxes Xenon, polishing his armor with his forearm.

Pointing his clenched fist at the field, Richard stood erect, "Here goes." The ruby in his ring flashed a brilliant red. "By the power of the transition elements, I summon the powers of chromium!" Sparks leapt into the air and drifted to the lush grass carpet forming a molten silver liquid, which singed the meadow. The liquid chromium shimmered for an instant before erupting like a geyser forming an oval-shaped, highly polished chrome mirror. Embedded in the charred ground, the mirror reflected the sun's rays bouncing them into the thick smog.

The rays sliced through the pollution that blanketed the deathly quiet field. Rupturing the silence, a spine-tingling shriek pierced the boys' ears. Jamming their fingers into their throbbing ears, the two brothers stared wide-eyed at Ozzie Ozone emerging from the smog.

Clawing at his throat, Ozzie Ozone crouched under his tattered cloak in a futile attempt to shield himself from the ultraviolet rays. Twisting his ghoulish figure away from the mirror, the sinister molecule glared at the brothers through sunken eyes. His decaying, green skin hung loosely beneath the black shadows surrounding his eye sockets.

"I will haunt you for the remainder of your short lives. Don't ever close your eyes!" growled Ozzie Ozone, dropping to his knees. Raising his gnarled hands, he reached for the boys and disappeared.

"I guess we didn't get rid of him forever," Anthony said, staring at the darkened spot where Ozzie Ozone last knelt before vanishing.

"That is a correct assumption. He will return," said Xerxes Xenon, mopping his brow with the back of his hand.

"Hey, look, the smog is clearing," said Richard, pointing at the field. "And they're moving. They're not dead."

"Now that Ozzie Ozone is gone, there is not enough pollution to create the smog. Fortunately, we are far enough from the city's pollution, or the situation could be much worse. But they will need medical attention. There is a phone in the field house. Call nine-one-one."

"I've got it," said Richard, turning to sprint across the field. "Hey, my mirror is disappearing."

"That happens with any object you create with your ring. If you fail to make it disappear, then after a certain amount of time it will disintegrate. The larger the object, the shorter the time it will last. Your rings have limits to their power. Now call for help. There will be time for answering questions later."

Nodding his head, Richard trotted along the fence line and disappeared into the field house. Emerging from the brick structure, Richard waved and flashed a thumbs-up to his brother. Both boys converged on the field and assisted several of the confused and dizzy players. A distant, wailing siren split the air.

27

"I'll bet our sisters are having much more fun," proclaimed Anthony, kneeling over Arvis. "Why do we always face death while they splash around in the pool? Next time, I think I'll stay home where it's safe from all of these monsters."

"Wow, look at how many ambulances they sent!" yelled Richard, above the high pitched sirens. "It looks like we'll get our first ambulance ride. Thank goodness we won't be strapped to a stretcher. I hate being sick."

"Me, too."

# "Hospital of Horrors"

"Doctor Ray, please report to the emergency room," blared the intercom.

"Mom, we're checking on Adrienne, Daina, and Tiffany," announced Jacqueline, waving to her mother.

"Girls, wait. Did the nurse say it was okay to visit them?"

"It'll be okay. The doctor said they could enter the rooms now. Walk to the end of the hall and turn left after passing under the radiology sign. They're in room two-oh-three," said the nurse, wearing a white dress and a name tag labeled "Christy, RN."

"Thank you, Christy. Okay, girls. I'm on my way to the first floor for a cup of coffee. I'll be back in a minute. Don't leave the second floor."

"We won't go anywhere," assured Catherine, leading the girls down the wide hospital corridor.

Passing a vacant stretcher parked against the wall, the girls paused under a sign etched with the word "Radiology." A woman in a green smock and a white lab coat raced past the girls. Slowly shuffling his slipper-covered feet, a man pushing a skinny metal rack on wheels crossed the hall in the opposite direction of the woman in the lab coat. A clear IV bag hung from the rack with a thin drip tube running from the IV bag to the man's arm. A slender man wearing spectacles and a blue lab coat rushed around the corner and crashed into Catherine.

Gathering himself, he addressed the girls harshly, "Why are you children standing in the middle of the hall? No one

29

under the age of eighteen is allowed up here without adult supervision. This is not a playground."

"They're with me," said Christy, wrapping her arm around Jeanne-Marie's shoulders.

"Well, get them out of the way. They're an accident waiting to happen."

The thin man straightened his spectacles and glared at the girls through narrowed, beady eyes. A thick vein running vertically along the side of his broad forehead pulsated with every word. Thrusting his shoulders back, the man stroked his dark hair, slapped his clipboard against his leg, and briskly strutted into the distance.

"You'll have to excuse him. That's Dr. James. Don't pay any attention to him. I don't think he has ever been nice to anyone. He's always grouchy and strange, too."

"I see what you mean. What was the room number again?" asked Catherine, massaging her upper arm.

"Room two-oh-three. It's to the left, three doors down."

"Okay, thanks."

"No problem, see you girls later."

The three girls looked both ways and cautiously stepped into the hall. Turning left, they approached room two-oh-three. The door was open.

"Catherine, Jacqueline, Jeanne-Marie, I'm glad to see you. I have a splitting headache. Come in, come in!" said Tiffany, motioning for the three sisters to enter the room. "Adrienne and Daina are sleeping. The nurse gave them a shot."

"Are they doing better?" asked Catherine, approaching the edge of Tiffany's bed.

"Yeah, they're on the other side of that blue curtain. We'll live. Although, for a while I had my doubts."

"I can only imagine. I think I'm ready to die when I catch a cold. I don't know what I would do if I felt as bad as you do."

"Let's hope it never happens again. The doctor said it was chlorine gas poisoning. Supposedly it was a fluke pool accident. They're still not sure what caused the chlorine gas leak. I..."

A knock at the door interrupted Tiffany.

"Excuse me, girls. I don't mean to barge in, but it's time for me to check on the patient. You can come back in about thirty minutes," said the nurse, stepping into the room and removing an inflatable cuff attached to a gauge from her coat pocket. A stethoscope hung loosely from her neck.

"What's that thing in your hand?" asked Jacqueline, quizzically eyeing the apparatus.

"Is that the thing you put around your arm and blow up to measure someone's blood pressure?" answered Catherine.

"That's right," replied the nurse. "This thing is actually called a sphygmomanometer. I know it's quite a mouthful, but that's its official name."

"Wow, cool. Thanks, huh, Nurse?"

"Call me Amy, and if you need anything just let me know."

"Thanks, Amy. We'll see you later," said Catherine, guiding her sisters out of the room.

"Bye," she answered, smiling.

"What should we do for half an hour?" asked Jacqueline, running her fingers through her strawberry-blond hair.

"I don't know. I don't see Mom," said Catherine, leading the girls through the hall and pausing once more under the radiology sign.

"I wish we could put on our glasses, but there are too many people wandering around," said Jacqueline, unwrapping a stick of gum.

"Jacqueline, you can't eat in here."

"I'm not eating. It's only a piece of gum. I'll only chew it, not eat it."

"I think the sign said no gum, too, Miss Smarty Pants. Mom won't be happy."

"I didn't want to chew it now anyway. Speaking of Mom, where is she?" asked Jacqueline, wrapping the gum and shoving it into her pocket.

"Getting coffee," answered Jeanne-Marie, watching her older sister cross her arms, stick out her lower lip, and turn her back on Catherine.

"We know that... Hey, she must be in the cafeteria."

"Yeah, I think it's on the first floor. Let's take the stairs," suggested Catherine, walking up the hall and opening a door to the stairwell. Descending the first flight of steps, Catherine stopped abruptly and grabbed the railing.

"What?"

"Shhh, listen. It sounds like that mean doctor," whispered Catherine, peering over the railing. "It's him!"

The three girls stared intently at Dr. James who spoke with a short, plump man in a plaid shirt. The stranger wore a black baseball cap pulled low over his eyes. His large, hairy hand was wrapped around the stair railing.

"I don't want to hear any more excuses. Do you have the money?" asked Dr. James, stuffing both hands in his coat pockets.

"Yeah, I brought it," answered the man, gruffly. "Here, it's all there." Removing an envelope from his pocket, the short man thrust it against the doctor's chest.

"Easy, this is no place to be hostile," said Dr. James, removing his right hand from his coat pocket and clutching the envelope. "Meet me in room four-twenty tonight, and I'll have it ready for you. These should do for now."

Dr. James removed a small package from his left coat pocket and handed it to the man with the baseball cap.

"Same time as usual?" asked the short man, concealing the package under his flannel shirt.

"No, let's make it eight-thirty instead."

"I'll be there."

"I know you will."

Without replying, the short man limped down the stairs favoring his right leg. Patting his coat pocket, Dr. James glanced up the stairs. The three girls held their breath and clutched the railing. Before they could move, the door behind them swung open.

"Hey, what are you doing in here?" asked Christy, holding the door open.

"Uuh... Looking for the cafeteria," said Jacqueline, exhaling sharply.

"Oh, it's down these stairs and to the right. Would you like me to show you?"

Peeking over the railing, Catherine quickly searched the stairs. Dr. James had vanished. "We... we can find it. Thanks."

"Okay. Hey, next time use the elevators or the stairs at the end of the hall. These are reserved for hospital employees. I don't want you to get in trouble. See you later."

"Bye, we'll use the other stairs like you said."

The three girls entered the hall and waited for the door to close behind them. Staring blankly at one another, the sisters meandered down the hall, each buried in her thoughts contemplating what they had witnessed.

"Catherine, girls," yelled Anthony, pursued by his older brother.

"Anthony, what are you doing here?" asked Catherine, turning to face him. Jeanne-Marie excitedly tackled her brothers.

"Everything's good," Richard said, affectionately patting Jeanne-Marie's head. "Ollie Oxygen told us about your meeting with Clifton Chlorine."

"Yeah, wow, that sounded scary," said Anthony. "But wait until you hear about Ozzie Ozone. That's really scary! He sent our whole football team to the hospital. I thought we were going to die. Xerxes Xenon and Richard's ring saved us, but Ned Nitrogen is hurt. Caspar Calcium is working on him."

"We'll tell you all about it. Mom said you could stay with us. Come on, we need to catch up with the elements. Clifton Chlorine is loose in the hospital, and he's looking for you."

# "Element Hospital"

"Where are we going?" asked Catherine, peeking into each room they passed.

"To the basement," replied Richard, ushering his sisters toward the stairs.

"Why?"

"The elements are waiting for us."

"Oh..."

"Wait, we're not supposed to use the stairs," said Jeanne-Marie, backing away from the door to the stairway.

"What? Said who?" asked Anthony, pushing Jeanne-Marie toward the door.

"It's okay," said Jacqueline, winking. "The nurse said we could use the stairs at the end of the hall. We're not supposed to use those other stairs."

"Some of the things you girls say make me wonder what you were doing before we caught up with you," said Richard, opening the door.

"Oh, nothing," responded Catherine, hurriedly. "Oh, okay. I admit I can't keep a secret. Actually, we did bump into a rude doctor. I think the nurse said his name was Dr. James. Anyway, a little later, we saw him talking to a scary looking guy on the stairs."

"Yeah it looked like a drug deal," blurted Jacqueline, bouncing down the steps. "And, they're going to meet at eight-thirty tonight in room four-twenty."

Anthony cautiously glanced over his shoulder. "Shhh, don't yell. We don't want the whole hospital to know about this."

"Hey, let's sneak over there later. I think we have to spend most of the night here anyway." Catherine's eyes sparkled with excitement. "Let's not tell the elements about this for now. They probably wouldn't want us to go."

"I don't know. It could be dangerous."

"Come on, haven't you always wanted to solve a mystery like in all those books in the library?"

The five children paused at the bottom of the stairs and exchanged anxious expressions. Catherine, trembling, flashed a crooked smile. With quick sweeping motions, she rubbed the goose bumps popping up on her arms. Richard and Anthony silently observed their sister and nodded knowingly.

"We'll do it!" said Richard. "How much more dangerous could it be than running into Ozzie Ozone. Speaking of Ozzie Ozone, we'd better get moving!"

Anthony eased open the door and peered into the hall. "Don't make too much noise. We're not supposed to be down here. The elements are in the storage room across the hall."

"What's in the storage room?" asked Jeanne-Marie, teasing the ends of her hair.

"A bunch of old computers and hospital equipment...and Element Hospital," answered Richard, with a sly smile.

"What's Element Hospital?"

"It's a hospital for the elements. They're operating on Ned Nitrogen and a few other elements. I think Ned Nitrogen will get better even though Ozzie Ozone almost killed him."

"How do they fit the hospital in one room?"

"How many questions are you going to ask? You'll see it in just one second. The elements don't need much room. Don't you remember how small they are?"

"Oh yeah..."

"The coast is clear. Come on, hurry!" urged Anthony, throwing open the door and walking briskly across the hall. Opening the door, Anthony hustled his brother and sisters into the storeroom. "Put on your glasses. The elements said no one comes in here until the end of the year to take inventory. The door is usually locked, but the elements unlocked it for us."

The five children quickly donned their glasses. Looking through the glasses, the once dimly lit, cluttered room seemed illuminated in hues of vibrant blue and yellow. Catherine and her sisters gawked at the miniature beds arranged in a circle in the middle of the room. Only two of the beds were occupied. A somber, bearded element clothed in a white robe stood in the middle of the circle. Caspar Calcium spoke softly with the whiskered element who prudently ran his fingers along the large "K" sewn into his robe.

Ned Nitrogen rested on the bed near Caspar Calcium. A small blue element with no cape and the letter "N" on his chest slept in the bed next to Ned Nitrogen. Three shimmering rays extended from the mysterious little element's arm and wrapped around Ned Nitrogen's arm like IV tubes.

"It's about time you appeared," grumbled Xerxes Xenon, standing with his hands firmly planted on his hips. "Ollie Oxygen could no longer wait for your arrival. Ozzie Ozone and Clifton Chlorine could be anywhere in the hospital. We have to find them before they find us. We even had to create a temporary hospital in this rat-infested room to avoid any surprise visits from those scoundrels. Ned Nitrogen is in no shape to be moved around the hospital. I do not know if he will survive the surgical procedure."

"What do you mean he's not going to make it?" asked Catherine, observing Ned Nitrogen's motionless body.

"Do I have to spell it out for you? Ned Nitrogen may become deceased, perish, cease to exist, expire, die! Do you understand? I realize Ned Nitrogen and I had our differences. That is quite understandable considering I am a noble, and he is a common gas. But, all in all, he is a good fellow whose friendship I would deeply miss."

"Me, too," responded Catherine, shocked by Xerxes Xenon's emotional outpouring. "What's wrong with him?"

"That is what Caspar Calcium and Dr. Kevin P. Kalium are discussing. They have immobilized Ned Nitrogen by triple bonding him with another nitrogen element. Those three rays you see connecting Ned Nitrogen and the nitrogen element are bonds. Together Ned Nitrogen and the nitrogen element form the molecule $N_2$, which keeps Ned Nitrogen inert. That means he remains very stable. He will not react with any other elements surrounding him. If we can keep him stable long enough, Dr. Kevin Kalium may be able to cure Ned Nitrogen."

"Is the doctor an element guardian, too?" asked Anthony, shifting his weight from one foot to the other.

"Most definitely, he is a member of the alkali metals family. Do not tell me you have not heard about the element kalium. Kalium is not only essential for plant growth, but is important for humans and animals. It plays a part in metabolism, the process by which you change food into energy and new tissue."

"I still don't think I've heard of him."

"Oh, wait a minute. Kalium is the Latin name for potassium. That is what his middle initial, P, represents. You know him by the name potassium," remarked Xerxes Xenon, shaking his head. "Dr. Kalium, do you have a moment?"

Patting Caspar Calcium on the shoulder, Dr. Kevin Kalium casually turned to face Xerxes Xenon. "I only have a moment. I'm about to prep for surgery. The patient is triple-bond stabilized. Now is our best opportunity to move ahead with the procedure."

"I have only one question. Would it be acceptable for the human guardians to observe the operation?"

"Most definitely! I have heard about you, and I wish to commend you for the courage you have displayed under great adversity. I would be delighted for you to witness the surgery," said Dr. Kalium, motioning for the children to gather around Ned Nitrogen's bed.

"And you thought I used big words," whispered Xerxes Xenon, watching Dr. Kalium out of the corner of his eye. "Dr. Kalium is probably one of the most intelligent and most educated elements. Of course, he has not quite attained the intellectual level of the nobles."

"Did you say something, Xerxes Xenon?"

"Nothing at all doctor. I believe we are ready on our end."

"Excellent, Caspar Calcium will be assisting throughout the surgical procedure."

Donning a mask and gloves, Dr. Kalium and Caspar Calcium hunched over Ned Nitrogen's motionless form. The children, following Xerxes Xenon's lead, crowded around the bed. Exchanging anxious expressions, Anthony and Richard focused their attention on Dr. Kalium who drew a series of black lines across Ned Nitrogen's upper torso.

Setting aside the marker, Dr. Kalium tilted his head toward Caspar Calcium, "Scalpel!"

Lifting a cotton cloth to reveal a shiny display of stainless steel instruments, Caspar Calcium gingerly plucked a small, straight, thin-bladed knife from the assortment of polished surgical devices. Tentatively, Caspar Calcium extended the scalpel, handle first, toward Dr. Kevin Kalium. As he had a thousand times before, the doctor stretched his hand toward the scalpel and gently clutched the handle.

"Don't cut him!" shrieked Jeanne-Marie, startling Dr. Kalium causing him to drop the scalpel.

Catherine clamped her hand over her open mouth and stared wide-eyed at her younger sister. Except for the clanging of the steel knife against the cold tile floor, not a sound could be heard. Lowering his head and drooping his shoulders, Dr. Kevin Kalium released a long, slow sigh. For what seemed like an eternity, the doctor stood with his back to the children. Finally, he spun about on the heel of his elfish shoes and scrutinized Jeanne-Marie through discerning eyes. The young girl nervously fidgeted with the pink, rose zircon stone in her ring and gazed timidly at her feet.

Dr. Kalium stepped away from the surgical table and shuffled toward Jeanne-Marie. "I understand your concern for your friend. Nevertheless, I cannot help him if I can't work on his internal structure of electrons, protons, and neutrons. This procedure is no different from a human having heart surgery."

"So, you're not mad?" mumbled Jeanne-Marie, bashfully shifting her eyes to look at the doctor.

"No, I'm not angry. I understand how confusing this can be. Here is what I'm going to do. I will retrieve a new, sterilized scalpel, with no germs, from Caspar Calcium, and I will make a small incision along the lines I drew on Ned Nitrogen. He won't feel a thing because he is sleeping deeply and won't awaken. Then I will be able to fix what is broken inside of him. And you can watch the whole operation if you promise not to scream again. Okay?"

"Okay, I promise," swore Jeanne-Marie, pressing her index finger against her lips, motioning for silence.

Winking at Jeanne-Marie, Dr. Kevin Potassium Kalium returned to his patient.

Once again the doctor addressed Caspar Calcium, "Scalpel!"

Caspar Calcium selected a razor-edged knife from the rows of stainless steel instruments and passed it to Dr. Kalium. With measured, controlled strokes the doctor masterfully removed the large N from Ned Nitrogen's chest. Bright spectral lines of light shot across the opening in Ned Nitrogen's chest.

"Wow, what's that?" inquired Jacqueline, stepping closer to the operating table.

"Why isn't he bleeding?" asked Catherine.

"Elements are not like humans. We do not have blood, but elements make up the blood in humans. Remember, elements are the simplest pure form of matter and are the building blocks for everything you see," lectured Xerxes Xenon, dramatically sweeping his arm in a wide arc. "However, elements, like humans, contain smaller particles. That is what you see in Ned Nitrogen."

"Particles? What particles? All I see is a bunch of lights flashing," noted Anthony, peering into the surgical hole in Ned Nitrogen's upper body.

"Those flashing lights, as you refer to them, are electrons, negatively charged particles in atoms. Elements contain

41

energy levels or shells through which the electrons move. This space, through which the electrons move, is called an orbital like the planets orbiting around the sun."

"Spectroscope," ordered Dr. Kalium. "We need to take a closer look at the electron energy levels."

"I agree," answered Caspar Calcium, lifting a long, slender tube, resembling a telescope and handing it to Dr. Kalium. "There appears to be a strange lump attached to his outer shell."

"I see it. Let's zoom in on that lump."

Clearing his throat, Xerxes Xenon glanced at Dr. Kalium as if offended by the doctor asking for the spectroscope, thus interrupting Xerxes Xenon's speech. "As I was saying, elements have many electron shells. In fact, the more electrons an element has, the more shells the element has because each shell holds only a certain number of electrons."

"Awesome! So what shell is that?" asked Richard, pointing at Ned Nitrogen's flashing lights.

"That is Ned Nitrogen's outermost shell, or principal energy level. The electrons in this outermost shell are referred to as valence electrons. Any element's outermost energy level can hold only eight electrons."

"How many electrons does Ned Nitrogen have?" asked Anthony.

"I can't believe you don't know that," exclaimed Jacqueline, shaking her head at her older brother. "Don't you remember the periodic table and how each element has an atomic number that tells you how many electrons and protons the element has? It's the big number in the element's square in the table. Remember, Holly Hydrogen is number one. So she only has one electron and one proton."

"Excellent. You might one day be worthy of the noble class. As Jacqueline surmised, that number, the atomic number, tells you exactly how many electrons the element has. Ned Nitrogen has seven electrons because his atomic number is seven."

"Cool, then all of Ned Nitrogen's electrons fit with room to spare," stated Anthony, straightening his shoulders in a scholarly manner.

"I'm afraid it is not that simple. Remember, this is Ned Nitrogen's outer shell. Most elements have many electron energy levels. Granted, a simple element such as hydrogen, which possesses only one electron, has only one level. On the other hand, Ned Nitrogen has two shells. The first shell, which is the most stable because it is closest to the element's nucleus, or heart if an element was human, can hold only two electrons. That leaves Ned Nitrogen five electrons for the second, outermost shell."

With his face glowing crimson, Anthony shifted his feet and bashfully shrugged his shoulders. Gathering himself, Anthony bent at the waist and peered closely at Ned Nitrogen, "He smells good. What cologne is he wearing?" Releasing a guttural laugh, Anthony stared giddily through glazed eyes.

"Are you crazy? What are you talking about? This isn't funny," scolded Richard, glaring at his brother.

"I can... can't help it. He..." Snorting uncontrollably, Anthony could no longer suppress his laughter. Grabbing his side, the young teenager doubled over at the waist, inhaling deeply.

For the first time, Xerxes Xenon stood speechless. Even Dr. Kalium and Caspar Calcium turned their attention from

43

the patient to Anthony. With her jaw dropped open, Catherine and her sisters watched their brother.

"I'm telling you..." Pausing once again to erupt in a fit of laughter, Anthony grinned crazily. "This fragrance is sweet. You've got to smell this..."

Casting a crooked smile toward the stunned onlookers, Anthony sleepily shook his head. Yawning, he desperately blinked his droopy eyelids. Opening his mouth, the thirteen-year-old attempted to speak, but he could only mouth words incomprehensibly. He stood silently for a moment. Then his head snapped backward and Anthony slumped against a shelf cluttered with damaged defibrillators. Before anyone could make an attempt to catch him, Anthony collapsed onto a heap of ragged blankets piled on the floor.

"Anthony, wake up!" cried Jeanne-Marie, clutching her head with her hands.

Racing to Anthony who lay sprawled on the floor, Caspar Calcium examined the boy. After a moment, Caspar Calcium turned to the startled group, "He's okay. He's sleeping soundly as if someone gave him an anesthetic. All we can do is let him sleep it off."

Climbing a nearby rack of shelves, Jacqueline located a green fire blanket. Unfolding the blanket, she draped it over her older brother. Richard found a wad of packaging foam and placed it under Anthony's head for a makeshift pillow.

"A pleasant odor..." pondered Dr. Kalium, focusing the spectroscope on Ned Nitrogen. "Of course, that's it. It's the lump. Look here."

Caspar Calcium peered through the spectroscope and nodded.

"In Ned Nitrogen's battle with Ozzie Ozone, he formed a bond with an oxygen atom. Ozzie Ozone must have pounded

him with a burst of ozone and electricity. Then, when we connected him with the nitrogen atom through these bonds to stabilize him, we formed the molecule $N_2O$, nitrous oxide. Our first step, before proceeding any farther into Ned Nitrogen's internal structure, is to remove this oxygen atom."

"I'm confused," said Catherine, blankly glancing at her brother and then back to Ned Nitrogen.

"Two nitrogen elements connected with an oxygen element forms the molecule $N_2O$, nitrous oxide. Your dentists call it laughing gas. It's an anesthetic. When Anthony moved too close to Ned Nitrogen, he inhaled the laughing gas and passed out." Xerxes Xenon paused and adjusted his crown. "In nature, oxygen and nitrogen form a direct union due to lightning during a thunderstorm. Recall ozone molecules have three oxygen atoms, $O_3$; somehow, one of Ozzie Ozone's oxygen atoms combined with Ned Nitrogen when Ozzie Ozone blasted him."

"So that's all that's wrong with him?" blurted Catherine.

"Unfortunately, there may be much worse damage. Dr. Kalium has only observed his outer shell. If Ned Nitrogen was a noble, that oxygen element would have never combined with his valence electrons. Noble gases have all eight valence electrons. Therefore, our outer shell is much more stable, and we will not easily combine with other elements. There is no room in our outer shell for another element's electrons to attach. Most common elements either combine with another element to fill their outer shell, or they give away their valence electrons to another element," stated Xerxes Xenon, egotistically. "We nobles are flawless. All other elements combine with one another to try to be like us."

46

"Hmm... Flawless," snipped Caspar Calcium. "Maybe, you should check that flawless physique of yours in the mirror."

"Like you have room to talk," retorted Xerxes Xenon. "Look at you strutting around with no shirt half the time. And those hideous tattoos. How barbaric! We nobles properly attire ourselves in royal garments for each occasion..."

"Silence, this is an operating room, not a nursery. You are upsetting the patient and me. I need to concentrate, and I cannot do that amidst such mindless chatter," scolded Dr. Kevin Potassium Kalium.

"Sorry," mumbled Caspar Calcium, exchanging agitated glances with Xerxes Xenon.

"Umm... Pardon me. Why would an element give up his electrons?" asked Richard, struggling to remember if he had learned about this in one of his science classes.

"To form an ionic bond," answered Caspar Calcium. "There are two ways an element can connect with another element: either through an ionic bond or through a covalent bond. In a covalent bond, the elements share electrons like in the triple covalent bond between Ned Nitrogen and the nitrogen element. In an ionic bond, one of the elements transfers its valence electrons to the other element."

"Thank you, Caspar Calcium, but you need to pay attention to assisting the good doctor," interrupted Xerxes Xenon.

Caspar Calcium turned toward Xerxes Xenon, pointing a clenched fist at him. Shaking his head, Caspar Calcium uncurled his fingers, releasing his clenched fist. Without further hesitation, he turned his back on Xerxes Xenon and directed his attention to the patient. Catherine thought she heard Caspar Calcium mutter something about Xerxes Xenon not being worth his time. Focused on his lecture to

Catherine and her siblings, Xerxes Xenon remained oblivious to Caspar Calcium's antics.

"I will handle the tutoring. Now, young ones, the whole purpose of forming bonds is to completely fill your shell to become more stable. That way, one avoids becoming too reactive and unstable, like someone with a short temper. Elements always fill their inner energy level, which holds two electrons, first because it is closest to the element's nucleus, which holds the protons and neutrons. Everyone wants to have the most protection and stability near their nucleus, even humans. That is why you have a rib cage to protect your nucleus consisting of your heart, lungs, and other vital organs. I am always stable and..."

"Xerxes Xenon, could you give us a moment of silence? No one can concentrate with your constant babbling," grumbled Dr. Kevin Kalium. "Torch and striker, please."

Xerxes Xenon started to reply but evidently thought it better to remain silent. Catherine figured this would be the best time to ask a question since someone other than Xerxes Xenon would probably answer it. With someone else answering the question, the answer would have to be much shorter and easier to understand. Looking one last time at Xerxes Xenon to assure he was not preparing to resume his lecture, Catherine scooted closer to Dr. Kevin P. Kalium.

"Why do you need a torch?" asked Catherine, scratching her head.

"If you heat nitrous oxide, $N_2O$, it will decompose or separate into oxygen and nitrogen. If I had a laser, I could heat the area around the oxygen atom without using the torch. Unfortunately, in this crude hospital we are forced to resort to more primitive methods."

"Separating molecules into elements is a chemical change," interjected Xerxes Xenon hastily. "Just like when an electric current is sent through water causing electrolysis, which separates $H_2O$, the chemical symbol for water, into its elements of hydrogen and oxygen."

"I know I did not just hear Xerxes Xenon's voice again," said Dr. Kalium, retrieving a striker from Caspar Calcium.

"Of course not, Doctor, there is nothing but tranquil silence over here. Please resume."

Dr. Kevin P. Kalium grumbled softly to Caspar Calcium, but Catherine could not understand what he said. Flicking the striker and adjusting the knob on the torch, Dr. Kalium lit the burner. Deftly maneuvering the torch's flame around the lump bulging from under Ned Nitrogen's outer shell, the doctor intently watched his patient's vital signs. The flashing lights zipped faster and faster across the opening. A slow hissing, resembling the sound of escaping gas, came from the lump.

"Ice, ice, he's heating too quickly! At this rate, he'll transform into a liquid state within minutes."

"That would be a physical change to go from a solid to a liquid," whispered Xerxes Xenon.

In the confusion and panic, no one paid attention to Xerxes Xenon's remark. Caspar Calcium frantically snatched a bag of shaved ice from a miniature cooler below the surgical table. The hissing grew louder. Dr. Kalium centered the torch's flame directly above the bubbling lump. Electrons streamed across the outer shell at blinding speeds becoming a blur. A series of spasms jolted Ned Nitrogen's body, leaving him trembling. Another loud hiss spurted from the lump. The patient quivered more violently. With a loud pop, the lump exploded, leaving a thin trail of gas rising to the ceiling.

"Ice him!" yelled Dr. Kalium, extinguishing the torch.

Flinging the bags on the table, the doctor and his assistant scrambled to cover Ned Nitrogen with ice. The patient lurched upward. Caspar Calcium grasped Ned Nitrogen's arms and restrained him against the bed. After another flurry of seizures racked his body, Ned Nitrogen fell immobile.

"He will be okay. I hope we've made it through the worst of the surgery. We need to probe a little farther into his energy sublevels and nucleus to make certain there is nothing else wrong with Ned Nitrogen."

"Energy sublevels?" asked Catherine, peering at the stationary Ned Nitrogen.

"Every electron energy level has sublevels or subshells. There are four possible sublevels, depending on how many electrons the energy level can hold. These sublevels are known as sharp, principal, diffuse, and fundamental; but everyone calls them s, p, d, and f. Only nobles use the sublevels' proper names," stated Xerxes Xenon, glowering at Dr. Kalium who rolled his eyes. "Anyway, Ned Nitrogen has two principal electron energy levels and each of these two energy levels has smaller sublevels. His outer energy level has two sublevels, s and p; his other energy level has one sublevel, s."

"How do you know how many sublevels he has?"

"Every element's energy levels has the same number of sublevels. The first energy level, the one closest to the nucleus, always has one sublevel. The next energy level has two sublevels; the next one has three sublevels, and so on. The s level can hold as many as two electrons, the p level holds up to six electrons, the d level can hold as many as ten electrons, and the f level can contain fourteen electrons."

"Oh... I see..." mumbled Catherine, attempting to make sense of the numbers and sublevels rattling inside her head.

"It's quite simple. Ned Nitrogen has seven electrons. His first energy level has one sublevel, s, which can hold two of the electrons. Seven minus two is five. Thus, we move to the next energy level, which has two sublevels, s and p. We place two electrons in the s sublevel in the outer shell. Five minus two is three. Therefore, we place the remaining three electrons in the p sublevel since it can hold up to six electrons. Those five electrons in the outer shell are then known as valence electrons. See, I told you it was elementary. These are only the basics of element structure..."

"How's he doing?" asked Ollie Oxygen, stepping in front of Xerxes Xenon who scowled at Ollie Oxygen. "Excuse me. As you would phrase it, I did not intend to bluntly interject."

"Sir, are you mocking me?"

"Don't be ridiculous, Xerxes Xenon. All I'm concerned with is Ned Nitrogen's health."

"He is improving," said Dr. Kalium. "His electron shells are in order. Kids, an easy way to remember the energy levels is to look at the periodic table. The first two columns, or groups, are the s level and the last six columns are the p level. The transition metals in the middle are the d level and the two rows at the very bottom with the actinides and lanthanides are the f levels. Now, we are examining the heaviest part of Ned Nitrogen, his nucleus. We need to make certain he has the correct number of neutrons. He has no charge, meaning he has seven negatively charged electrons and seven positively charged protons. A negative seven plus a positive seven equals zero leaving Ned Nitrogen with no charge, or neutral. Therefore, he remains stable as he should be," noted Dr. Kalium, peering through the spectroscope. "Did you find Clifton Chlorine or Ozzie Ozone?"

"Yes. Fortunately, neither one of those villains has found the other. They're both boiling with rage, and it's only a matter of time before one of them explodes. We have to stop them soon before someone gets hurt. What happened to Anthony? Why is he lying on the floor? Is he tired?"

Suppressing a giggle, Jeanne-Marie blurted, "He smelled laughing gas and went nighty-night. It's an ane... anes..."

"Anesthetic," said Xerxes Xenon, completing the young girl's sentence. "Ozzie Ozone managed to bond an oxygen atom to Ned Nitrogen, turning him into the molecule nitrous oxide."

"Laughing gas. How clever. Ozzie Ozone will be extremely difficult to apprehend. What is his weakness?" pondered Ollie Oxygen, thoughtfully stroking his chin.

"Trees, especially pines and oaks, absorb ozone," replied Richard, beaming proudly.

"True, but we don't have enough trees in the hospital to do Ozzie Ozone any harm."

"He is not radioactive," said Dr. Kalium, straightening from bending over the patient.

"Ozzie Ozone isn't radioactive?" asked Catherine, twisting the end of her hair around her finger.

"No, Ozzie Ozone isn't radioactive. But I was referring to Ned Nitrogen. His nucleus is stable. The nucleus of a stable element contains as many neutrons as protons or more. Ned Nitrogen's atomic weight or mass is correct at fourteen AMU's. We use atomic mass units rather than pounds because we are so light..."

"Actually, one atomic mass unit is one-twelfth the mass of carbon twelve," interjected Xerxes Xenon, smiling smugly.

"Anyway, if you subtract his atomic number of seven from his atomic mass of fourteen, you will discover Ned

Nitrogen should have seven neutrons. And there were exactly seven neutrons in Ned Nitrogen's nucleus. It appears there was no damage to his core structure. What a relief. If you're ready, Caspar Calcium, we'll stitch the patient," said Dr. Kalium, triumphantly.

"Ned Nitrogen is going to be all better!" cheered Jeanne-Marie, clapping her hands.

"I believe so. He'll need rest though," said Caspar Calcium, threading a needle. "And I apologize for losing my temper earlier. I believe everyone was a little on edge since we were all concerned with Ned Nitrogen's health. I sense the tension in the room has eased. What do you think Xerxes Xenon?"

"Hmf..." snorted Xerxes Xenon, not wanting to admit to having to agree with Caspar Calcium.

"Great, then he'll be okay. Wow, that was a long operation!" stated Catherine, searching for a clock. "What time is it?"

"Eight o'clock."

"Eight o'clock. It's late. We have to go," said Catherine, eyeing her brother and sisters.

"Go where?" asked Jeanne-Marie.

Shrugging bashfully, Catherine glared at her sister out of the corner of her eye. "Remember what we talked about around room four-twenty."

"Oh, yeah, the mystery with the mean..."

"Right, you mean we need to meet with the doctor on our way to see Mom," interrupted Jacqueline, draping her arm around Jeanne-Marie's shoulder and directing her toward the door.

"What about Anthony?"

"Anthony will wake soon, and I'll have him meet you and your mom. Laughing gas is a mild anesthesia, which doesn't last long. In fact, it usually won't even put you to sleep unless you inhale too much of it like Anthony managed to do. Anyway, when he wakes, I'll tell him where you went. I don't want you to get in trouble with mom. You are going to see your mom, right?" questioned Ollie Oxygen, observing the children suspiciously.

The four youngsters nodded hurriedly and shuffled toward the door. Glancing once more at Ned Nitrogen and the two surgeons hovering over him, Richard and his sisters paused. Then waving, the children exited the room stepping into the hallway.

# "Room 420"

"Here it is, room four-twenty," exclaimed Jacqueline, pointing to the mahogany door. "These are nice offices. I like the thick carpet. I could take a nap out here." Jacqueline stooped and patted the rich, ornamental wall-to-wall carpet.

"This has to be the executive wing," commented Richard, observing the marble walls and plush Victorian-style furniture. "The hospital director's office must be that big one at the end of the hall. I would like to work up here."

"I guess everyone went home," observed Catherine, scanning the vacant hall. "I wonder where Dr. James is. Where should we hide? I don't want him to catch us."

Nodding vigorously, Jacqueline agreed with her sister. "Me, neither. I don't see any place to hide out here."

"What about in here?" asked Jeanne-Marie, twisting the knob on the door to room four-twenty and flinging it open.

"Oh my... Jeanne-Marie, you can't just open doors like that. What if Dr. James had been in there? We'd have been in serious trouble," scolded Catherine, peering into the dark office. "Oh, well, now that you have it open, we might as well investigate. This is spooky. I've got chills running down my spine."

"Me, too," stated Jacqueline, staring into the vacant room but hesitating to enter it.

"Come on, we can't stand here. We don't have much time before Dr. James arrives. From the way you described him, I'd hate to get caught half-way between his office and the hall," said Richard, leading his sisters into the office. "What are we looking for?"

"I don't know. I guess anything illegal. Like drugs," whispered Catherine, flicking on the desk lamp.

"Real good, Catherine. This is a hospital. Of course, he's going to have drugs in here."

"Oh, yeah. Hey, maybe we'll find a note or some other incriminating evidence."

"Incriminating evidence? That's some fancy terminology. I think you've been reading too many mystery novels. But I doubt we'll find any evidence that could be used to accuse the doctor of a crime."

The four children surveyed the small office. An enormous, uncluttered desk, a large, overstuffed leather chair, and two smaller, exquisitely upholstered chairs filled the office to capacity. Trimming out the room was a window concealed behind a set of Venetian blinds and an unidentified side door.

"I'll check the closet," said Jeanne-Marie, opening a mahogany-stained door. "Look, it's another room."

"It's a conference room. I doubt you'll find anything in there, but you can check it out. I'll go with you." Richard and Jeanne-Marie entered the conference room closing the door behind them.

"Wow," exclaimed Jacqueline, lifting an envelope from the desk's top drawer. "There must be ten thousand dollars in here. Look at all of the hundred-dollar bills."

"Let me see that," said Catherine, snatching the envelope from her sister. "You're right. What else is in there?"

"Some pencils, pens, paper clips, rubber bands, DVDs, umm...uhhhh...."

"What is it?"

"There's... There's a... There's a gun in here!"

"Don't touch it. Maybe we should leave before it's too late. I'll get Richard and Jeanne-Marie."

"Catherine, wait. Do you hear voices?"

Both girls froze, listening intently. Two harsh, yet indistinguishable voices grew louder. Within seconds a shadow fell across the doorway. Stashing the cash in the drawer, turning off the desk lamp, and quietly shutting the drawer, Catherine dragged her sister under the desk.

"Who left the door open?" asked Dr. James, stepping lightly into the room.

Heavy steps vibrated across the office floor. "Maybe it was the janitor," suggested a gruff voice.

"They aren't supposed to clean the offices until tomorrow. I need to get the lock fixed for my door," muttered Dr. James, clicking on the desk lamp. "Have a seat, Jim."

"So, Doc, did you bring the goods?" asked Jim, his immense weight causing one of the office chairs to creak.

"Oh, yes, I brought you more than you could ever imagine. But first I want to make a few things clear," stated Dr. James, moving around the desk.

Catherine and Jacqueline held their breath. Seized with panic, the girls stared at the doctor's saddle-oxford wingtips, inches from where they huddled. His tailored, cuffed slacks neatly rested over the tops of his shoes. The girls could hear the desk drawer slowly roll open.

"Lately, Jim, you've disappointed me. You've become too brusque in muscling your way around here. This is a professional setting, considering we are in a hospital. The last thing we want is to raise suspicion."

"That's your problem. You're the one who doesn't want to come downtown. You're afraid to leave your cozy neighborhood. You're afraid to face the real world. I'm the one who's doing you a favor. If things are too hot for you, I can find another doctor."

"No, that won't be necessary. Maybe we should simply lay low for a while."

"Lay low? Since when does the world revolve around you, Doc? I have clients waiting. Do you think they want to lay low until it's convenient for you? Now, are you in or out?"

"I... I just need a week. That's all."

"You know what that answer says to me? It says you're out."

Trembling, the girls heard the chair creak and heavy steps shuffle toward the desk. The doctor's polished shoes slid along the floor backing a couple of inches away from the desk. The sisters struggled to remain motionless taking slow, measured breaths. Sweat beaded on their foreheads and upper lips.

"And you know the only way out, don't you, Doc? Too bad you didn't make some friends around here. I doubt anyone will even miss you. But when they finally discover your absence, I'd be amazed if anyone even looks into your whereabouts. You'll simply disappear."

"No. No, I don't want out. How about a couple of days? I've been your most dependable source."

"Maybe, but doctors are a dime a dozen. Medical schools pump them out faster than we can find new clients. You're replaceable. This is your last chance. Hand me the goods, and I'll forget we even had this little conversation, or you're out. Your move, Doc."

"Interesting situation we have here. Isn't it, girls?" asked a small, yellow element with a yellow-green cape and a "Cl" on his chest. "Did you forget about your pal, Clifton Chlorine? I sure hope not. I'll probably be the last element the two of you ever see. This is so much fun. I can't decide if I should take care of you myself or let the doctor and his business partner handle it. Of course, I can't wait to hear the doctor's answer to Jim's question considering he doesn't even have the goods Jim wants. Don't look so shocked. Those two can't see or hear me, but they can definitely hear you scream."

"Well, Doc," snarled Jim. "I don't have all night."

"Okay, I've got it right here," answered Dr. James.

The girls cringed watching the doctor's fingers wrap around the edge of the drawer. The scraping sound of metal dragging against wood startled Catherine who clutched her sister's arm too tightly. Jacqueline clamped her hand over her mouth to muffle her shriek and glared at her sister who released her vise-like grip.

"Now let's see who's expendable."

"Whoa, Doc. Take it easy. You know if you do anything rash others will come looking for me. And this will be the first place they search since they know this is the last place I visited."

"You can't talk your way out of this one, Jim. You've bullied me too much. Without me, you would have no operation. Just like you said, you can find other doctors; I can find other dealers. I've had enough of you. I don't like your slow-talking drawl, your ragged, sloppy attire, your thug-like demeanor, or the way you smell. Say good-bye, Jim."

"I'll ki..."

An ear-splitting explosion silenced Jim's outburst. Catherine and Jacqueline jumped bumping their heads against the under side of the desk. The girls' thumping against the desk was stifled by the crash of a heavy object hitting the floor.

With their ears pressed against the conference room door, Richard and Jeanne-Marie exchanged horrified looks. Desperately scanning the room, Richard spotted another door. Pointing to the opposite end of the room, Richard pressed his index finger against his lips and grabbed his sister by the arm. The siblings tiptoed across the carpeted floor stopping at the door. Slowly and meticulously grasping and turning the knob, Richard opened the door enough for him and Jeanne-Marie to squeeze through. Closing the door, the two scanned the small office.

"It's another office," whispered Richard. "There's another door. We've got to get the elements."

Following her brother to the next door, Jeanne-Marie asked, "Are Catherine and Jacqueline okay?"

"Yes, Dr. James or that Jim guy would have said something if they had found them," whispered Richard, clutching the doorknob. "It's locked."

• • •

A smile curled across Clifton Chlorine's yellow face. "You have to love humanity's cruelty. There's nothing better than human greed, rage, and cold-blooded brutality. You know, girls, I'm enjoying this so much that I don't feel like wasting the time or energy to dispose of you now. I want to follow our good doctor here to see what he has up his sleeve next. There's nowhere for you to go anyway. Besides, the doctor may yet discover your little hideout. I never thought a game of hide-and-seek could be so much fun. See you soon. And oh, don't scream."

Clifton Chlorine disappeared over the top of the desk. Catherine and Jacqueline drew their legs closer into their bodies and pressed themselves against the back of the desk as if they could disappear into the woodwork. Jacqueline wiped the sweat from her upper lip and closed her eyes. A lone tear trickled down her cheek.

The door to the office opened and then quickly closed. Rapid footsteps grew fainter as they moved farther and farther down the hall. Grabbing her sister's hand, Catherine dragged her from under the desk.

"Come on, Jacqueline, we have to get out of here."

For a moment, Jacqueline resisted before gathering herself and standing. Catherine stepped around the edge of the desk and froze staring at a large pair of workboot-clad feet protruding into her path. Afraid to approach the still body sprawled across the office floor, Catherine stood immobile.

Faint footsteps and the sound of squeaking wheels approached the office. Tapping Catherine on the shoulder, Jacqueline pointed to the entrance to the conference room. Both girls lunged for the passage, stumbling over each other. Jerking the door open, Catherine followed her sister into the dark room and shut the door after them. Resting against it, the two girls listened intently.

The office door burst inward crashing against the wall. The sound of wheels entered the office and stopped. Catherine and Jacqueline could barely understand the doctor's mumbling.

"Looks like we have a guest for the morgue. If goods are what you're looking for, then I think we've hit the jackpot. Don't you agree, Jim? What was that you said, Jim? I can't hear you. Oh, now you don't want to speak to me. Aren't we the quiet one tonight? I'm afraid the silent treatment won't change my mind. It's so quiet in here, you'd think someone had died," cackled Dr. James, laughing hysterically.

With a little more muttering and grumbling, the doctor strained against a heavy object. The girls heard continued grunting and panting followed by the squeaking of wheels. The thud of a heavy object and then the slamming of a drawer interrupted a moment of silence. Once again the wheels chirped loudly, resonating throughout the hall. The squeaking paused and the office door slammed shut. Then the chattering wheels resumed with the sound becoming less audible until it faded into the distance.

"I think he's gone," said Catherine, releasing a quivering sigh.

"Let's go before he gets back," urged Jacqueline, springing to her feet.

The far conference room door flew open. Catherine and Jacqueline gasped in terror. Two figures rushed inside.

"Catherine, Jacqueline, you got out," squealed Jeanne-Marie, running ahead of Richard.

"Don't do that again. You scared us to death," scolded Jacqueline, collapsing against the wall.

"Sorry."

"Hey, is that another way out?" asked Catherine, pointing to the other door.

"Yeah, it leads to another room. But the office door is locked," said Richard, shaking his head. "We heard everything and were trying to find a way out to get help."

"I can't believe he did that. He's crazy. Someone needs to lock him in an insane asylum and throw away the key."

"I know. We should never have gotten involved. This is way over our heads. Let's just get out of here."

"We can't let him get away with it. Whatever it is he's doing. I don't know what the goods are, but I do know we can get him for murder."

62

"That's great. What are you going to do, arrest him? You'll end up like Jim. I think we should get out of here and call the police."

"What can the police do? We don't have any evidence. Besides, we need to figure out what the goods are."

"Catherine... Hey, I forgot about our rings. We can use our element powers to protect us and to take him down. Let's do it. We need to find the body first."

"I heard him mutter something about the morgue," said Jacqueline, her eyes widening in excitement.

"I can't believe I forgot about my Ring of Enlightenment," said Catherine, rubbing the green emerald set in a golden band wrapped around her ring finger.

"We have to watch for Clifton Chlorine. I think he followed Dr. James," cautioned Jacqueline, opening the conference room door.

Richard and his three sisters slipped out of the conference room and into the doctor's office. All four children stepped around the opposite side of the desk careful to avoid the spot where Jim fell. Stepping into the hall, the foursome squinted under the bright fluorescent lights. Closing the door, Richard rubbed his ring against his shirt and breathed heavily. Transferring his attention to his siblings, he and his three sisters trotted down the hall. Rounding the corner, Richard collided with a thin figure and they fell to the floor.

"Don't move," yelled Jacqueline, holding her outstretched, ring-bearing hand before her.

"I wasn't planning on it. Take it easy. Ouch, my head," said Anthony, lifting himself off the floor.

"Oops, sorry about that," apologized Richard, helping his brother to his feet. "What are you doing up here?"

"When I awoke, Ollie Oxygen told me you were with Mom, but I remembered how you were planning to check out room four-twenty. So I ran up here to check things out. I just passed some doctor wheeling a stretcher with a body into the elevator. It looked like the guy was dead the way the doctor had him covered with a white sheet."

"He was dead. Come on, we're going to the morgue. I'll tell you about it on the way. You're not going to believe this."

## CHAPTER NINE
### Episode Eleven
# "The Morgue"

"There he is," Richard whispered, watching Dr. James turn left into an adjoining corridor.

"This is crazy," muttered Anthony. "This guy has a gun and evidently doesn't mind using it. I'm impressed with our rings' powers, but I doubt they can stop a bullet. Maybe we should think about this."

"No one said we're going to arrest him. We're simply looking for some evidence. We'll only use our rings in an emergency," whispered Catherine, peeking around the corner. "Hey, he went in that room. It must be the morgue."

"What do we do?" asked Jacqueline, sweeping her bangs from her face. "Won't he see us if we go in there?"

"There's a window in the door. We can peek in the room first."

Leaning against the wall, Richard pondered his sister's words. "Wait a minute. Jacqueline has a good point. Even if he doesn't see us go in the room, there's no way all of us can find a hiding place in there. Anthony, why don't you wait out here with Jacqueline and Jeanne-Marie, and Catherine and I'll check it out."

"Sounds good to me. Scream if you run into trouble and we'll show Dr. James what our rings can do. Maybe if enough of us charge into the room, we can overpower him," said Anthony, rubbing his ring's blue sapphire stone against his shirt. "We'll watch the hall in case anyone or anything should wander down here. I still don't think this is the greatest idea, so let's get it over with as soon as possible."

65

Annoyed, Catherine slapped her arms against her sides. "Okay, Anthony, we get the point. You're such a Boy Scout! Where's your sense of adventure? You're just like Mom. You worry too much."

"I'm not worried. I'm using common sense. By the way, common sense is something you can learn from the Boy Scouts. And anyone, even a Boy Scout, can tell you this is dangerous. One day you're going to end up in a situation you can't get out of. Wait a minute, what about the gun? That's definitely evidence. In fact, the police will even be able to tell that it was recently fired."

"True, but we need more than a gun. If we can't prove he shot this guy Jim, then the gun is useless. We need to catch him red-handed."

"You're crazy. How much more red-handed can you get? There's a gun in the office, a dead person in the morgue, and I'm sure there is blood on the carpet."

"You're right again, Anthony. But we need to catch him with the goods to really stop whatever it is he's selling illegally."

"I'll leave that to the police."

"They'll never get here in time. Dr. James will be gone, and we'll have a lot of explaining to do..."

"Quiet! We've made our decision. Anthony, are you in or out? Let's go, Catherine," whispered Richard, stepping between the feuding siblings.

Grabbing Catherine by the arm, Richard led her into the hall without waiting for Anthony's response. Brother and sister slid along the wall avoiding the center of the corridor. With each measured step, the morgue's double doors loomed ever closer.

Richard stopped and motioned for his sister to wait. Catherine nodded and glanced behind her, seeing her brother and two sisters peeping around the corner. Smiling, she jabbed her thumb in the air and pointed to her brother. Anthony rolled his eyes, nodded, and signaled with a thumbs-up.

Dropping to his knees, Richard crawled to the doors and slowly rose to his feet. Catherine edged closer to the entrance. Holding his hands before him and shrugging his shoulders, Richard turned from the door's window to his sister. Catherine slithered along the floor and stood beside her brother. The two exchanged worried looks and slowly pushed open the left door.

The biting odor of formaldehyde stole their breath. Richard stuffed his face into his shirt, and Catherine cupped her hand over her nose and mouth. Surveying the rows of stainless steel tables, Catherine relaxed, noting that the barren room lacked any cadavers. She rubbed her arm with her free hand and shuddered in the cold morgue.

"Psst, Catherine," whispered Richard, pointing to a light streaming from under a curtain that sectioned off the rear portion of the room.

The two children stood staring at the curtain through which they could barely discern the shape of a thin figure. The silhouette hunched over and then straightened. Bending once again the dark form continued with his work.

Catherine and Richard painstakingly crept along the tile walls to the curtain. The clatter of metal against metal rang from the other side of the cloth barrier. An ear-piercing whine erupted from a surgical saw tearing through bone and tissue. A foul odor permeated the air. Richard grabbed Catherine's arm and pulled her behind a stainless steel cart loaded with plastic containers.

"What are we going to do?" mouthed Richard, making no audible sound.

Shrugging, Catherine drew her legs to her chest and placed her head on her knees. Her face turned a ghostly pale, and she struggled against a sudden onrush of nausea. Lifting her head, Catherine stared dizzily at the thin shadow struggling with a large object resting on the outline of a table behind the curtain.

Richard rose to his feet, motioning for his sister to remain seated behind the cart. Reaching for the corner of the curtain, he hesitated. Once again the teenager cautiously stretched his hand toward the large drape as if reaching for the handle of a hot pot on the stove. This time he clutched the cloth material and opened it enough to peer into the area with one eye. Quickly releasing his grip and spinning around, Richard dropped to the floor holding his stomach.

Catherine stared at her bother's pale, green face and suddenly had no desire to know what was happening behind the curtain. *Maybe we should just forget about Dr. James, but how could we forget the incident that occurred in room four-twenty? Something has to be done. Don't they always say that justice must be served?* Catherine hung her head. A tear trickled down her cheek. She could not understand how someone, especially someone as respected as a doctor, could be so evil.

The doors to the morgue flew open shattering Catherine's thoughts. She and her brother clung to the cart wishing it was larger, but there was no other place to hide. Two men attired in green smocks sauntered into the room chatting loudly.

"Can you believe that overtime shot?" proclaimed the taller of the two men.

He sprang forward and flipped an imaginary ball toward the curtain concealing Dr. James. Landing in a crouched position, the tall man raised both arms and hopped around the vacant morgue. Wiping sweat from his brow, he smiled jubilantly.

"He's still the greatest," answered the other, running his hand over his short-clipped, dark hair.

"Hey, Ray, it looks like someone else is pulling a late shift," said the tall man, pointing to the silhouette hustling around the object behind the curtain.

"I don't remember seeing anyone else listed on the chart for tonight," commented Ray.

"Me neither. I thought we were the only poor saps logging extra hours on the graveyard shift."

"Dr. James, what are you doing here?" asked Ray, pulling open the curtain. "I didn't see you listed on the chart."

"The chart is for rookies," retorted Dr. James. "I don't report to anyone. Now if you'll excuse me, I'd like to wrap up here."

"Excuse us, doctor. But regulations have been established for the safety and efficiency of the hospital. You are not above the rules, and if you don't improve your attitude..."

"Look, Ray, I have more important things to do than concern myself with your idle threats. Besides, you're in no position to execute laws around here. I don't even see how you can call yourself a real doctor. What doctor allows himself to be referred to by his first name? Doctor Ray, sounds like a horse doctor. I'll bet no one at this hospital even knows your last name. You and your two years of medical experience, the nurses know more than you. In fact, if you knew anything, you would quickly ascertain I was in the process of delivering this donor's organs to the organ bank. Did you know organs deteriorate, or should I say die, outside the body if they are not kept cold?"

"I'll show you what to do with those organs, Doctor..."

"Forget it, Ray, he's not worth our time," said the tall man, stepping between Ray and Dr. James. "Come on, his time will come," continued the man, pushing Ray around the curtain and into the center of the room. "Let's make our rounds, and we'll come back when that clown has finished."

"Good idea. You'd better keep me away from that creep before I dot his eye."

"Don't think about it. Violence won't solve anything. It would probably get you suspended or even fired, especially since Doctor James has seniority. Let's get out of here."

"He ruined a perfectly good night," grumbled Ray, kicking the door open and exiting the room.

"Remember that patience thing you were working on?"

"Yeah."

"Now is the time to show me that patience. Come on, Noodle, you will live to fight another day, but we'd best do a little training first. I'd hate to see that old man whip you," shouted the tall man, his voice echoing throughout the hall. The two men's laughter drifted into the morgue.

Catherine and Richard exchanged puzzled, frightened expressions and crept from behind the cart. The curtain slid open, forcing the siblings to dive for shelter. Not wasting any time, Dr. James ran across the room lugging a Styrofoam cooler behind him. Brother and sister held their breath until he exited through the swinging doors.

"We're getting out of here," hissed Richard, clutching Catherine's arm and practically dragging her toward the doors.

"Slow down!" screeched Catherine, staggering behind her brother. "At least, let me catch my balance. You're not the only one who doesn't want to be in here. You can loosen your grip, too. You're cutting off the blood to my arm."

Richard failed to hear his sister's complaints. Rather, he concentrated on opening the door as quietly as possible. Cautiously, sticking his head into the hallway like a turtle peeking from his shell, Richard looked left and right, checking both ends of the passageway.

"Is it all clear?"

Spinning around, Catherine froze, confronting the mocking grin plastered across Clifton Chlorine's face.

"Yeah, I think it's safe," answered Richard, without looking at his sister. "I..."

Catherine stumbled over Richard's legs, knocking him into the hall. Falling beside her brother, she propped herself up on her hands and scooted across the floor like a crab until her back pressed against the wall. Richard clambered to his knees and frowned at his sister.

"What's wrong with you? Are you trying to kill me?"

"She's not, but I am," hissed Clifton Chlorine, zipping between the siblings. "We need to finish what we started in Dr. James office. In fact..."

"By the power of the transition metals, I summon titanium!" yelled Anthony, racing down the corridor with Jacqueline and Jeanne-Marie trailing after him.

A blue ray exploded from Anthony's ring. Streaking down the hallway, the beam slammed into Clifton Chlorine who erupted in a ball of smoke. Within seconds, the hall flooded with white smoke.

"Help. I can't see!" screamed Catherine. "Richard, where are you?"

"Help, help!" mocked Clifton Chlorine. "Of course, you can't see. Foolish runts, you don't know the first thing about the elements' powers. How naive you are. I've been waiting for a blast of titanium," snarled Clifton Chlorine, laughing hysterically. "Have you ever heard of titanium tetrachloride, or should I say titanium combined with chlorine? Oh, please, please let me answer this one. No, you haven't, otherwise you wouldn't have helped me create titanium tetrachloride, better known as a smoke screen. What are five blind mice going to do now?" gloated Clifton Chlorine, cackling with glee. "Peek-a-boo, I see you. How I wish you could see me. Oh, well, I guess you'll never see the approaching end of your worthless lives. Goodnight, kids, forever."

# CHAPTER TEN
## Episode Eleven

# "Dreams"

"We're not worthless," Jacqueline shouted. "By the power of the alkaline earth metals, I summon magnesium!" screamed the young girl, unleashing a brilliant purple spark.

The spark slashed through the smog, briefly illuminating the hall. Before the children could find one another, the smoke screen swallowed the purple flash. Clifton Chlorine's ghastly snickering broke the silence.

"You missed," he said. "I told you I wouldn't be taken so easily this time. You urchins were lucky at the swimming pool, but we're not at the pool anymore. How do you expect to hit me when you can't see me? Blind mice, blind mice stuck in the mouse trap," he sang. "Where are you going to run? Nowhere. Since we have this precious time together, let's play a little game. Do you like games?"

"Leave us alone!" screamed Catherine through a flood of tears.

"Alone, is that what you want? That's exactly what you'll get. You're our winner in the first round of fear, the game every child should play. You, my dear sniffling girl, get to go first. What are you afraid of-the dark, death, water, heights, snakes...hmmm? Oh, don't tell me. Rather, dry your tears and inhale my intoxicating fragrance. It will take you on a trip into your greatest fears. You will think it is real, but it will all be in your mind. You won't know the difference though, and that's why your fear will destroy you. Few ever truly conquer their fears; and if you also fail, you will never return to the real world. It's a pity your rings won't save you. I so enjoy

73

watching you pitiful humans writhe in agony, victims of your imagination. Enjoy. Breathe deeply, my sweetie."

"No!" choked Catherine, creeping frantically along the floor.

Clawing at the cold tiles, she scurried forward only to smack her head into the wall. Clutching the top of her head, she pulled herself into a fetal position. The pleasant odor of cranberry-scented candles drifted into her nostrils. Relaxing, Catherine rolled onto her back and inhaled vigorously.

"Come, boys and girls, join your sister," hissed Clifton Chlorine. "Look how peacefully she...oh, that's right, you can't see! How could I forget? At least, you still possess your other four senses, for the moment. Breathe freely and enter my dream world. Come, join me," he said, guffawing uncontrollably.

"Catherine, don't listen to him," cried Richard. "He can't..."

"You can't resist it. Don't even try. It is too late."

"It's okay," sighed Catherine. "I feel great. Look at the pretty colors. Wow, flowers are falling from the sky! Jacqueline, you have to see this. I can even pick them up. Cool! It's moving in my hand and changing shapes. That's not possible. This flower is growing legs. It's holding onto my thumb. Let go. Ah, it's a roach. The flowers...they're all bugs!" screamed Catherine. "Bugs, big bugs! They're crawling on me. Get them off! They keep falling from the sky. I can't stop them. I've got to get away. Why can't I move? Ahhh, they're in my hair. It's in my ear. Help...help me! I... I can't breathe!"

• • •

"Where did everyone go?" Jacqueline asked. "Hey, why is my cello here? When did I put on my pretty black dress? Mom made this for me to wear only during performances. I am in

so much trouble if she sees me in this dress. Where am I?" She gently fingered the silver sequins adorning the top of her dress. "Look, the black wall in front of me is moving. Wait, it's a curtain. Oh my gosh, I must have been daydreaming. I forgot about my solo tonight. Is it already Saturday? I know I get nervous before these shows, but I must have blacked out for a moment. Oh, I hope they like me. Please, don't let me mess up tonight," she prayed. "This chair is so uncomfortable. Where's my music? I can't play without my music. Did the rest of the orchestra disappear? Where are they?"

"Ladies and gentlemen, I give you tonight's guest soloist, Jacqueline," announced a voice from above.

The curtain slowly parted to reveal an auditorium teeming with adults and children. Jacqueline frantically adjusted her cello's endpin and drew her bow across the strings. A shrill squawk sounded.

"Who killed the chicken?" yelled a chubby kid in glasses.

The performance hall erupted in laughter. With trembling hands, Jacqueline positioned her fingers along the neck of her cello and once again drew her bow across the cello's large belly. The musical instrument emitted a high-pitched shriek, causing everyone in the front row to clamp their hands over their ears.

"Do you call yourself a musician?" shouted an elderly man, raising his walking cane above his head and shaking it at Jacqueline. "This is torture!"

"I'm sorry," mumbled Jacqueline, her face flushed red. "It must be out of tune."

"That's not the only thing out of tune," snapped an old lady, sitting beside the elderly gentleman with the cane. "Look at the way you're dressed. Do you not have any respect?"

"Do you not like my dress?" asked Jacqueline, bewildered.

"Your top looks like it was cut off a dress. But exposing your belly and legs is completely inappropriate, not to mention those ridiculous sunglasses."

"Wha...What? Oh my... no...What happened? Why am I wearing my running shorts? Who cut the top off my dress? It's so short, it won't even cover my stomach. I'm not even wearing any shoes," cried Jacqueline, hiding behind her cello.

"Boo," hissed the audience.

"Look, it's Jacqueline from school!"

"Adrienne, what are you doing in the audience? I thought you were supposed to be playing beside me."

"No way. I don't want everyone to think I'm a geek, too."

"What? You're my best friend."

"Are you crazy? Oh, I guess that was a dumb question. Just look at what you're wearing. You don't have any friends. No one likes you or your dumb glasses or that wild stringy hair."

"Why are you saying that?"

"You're just not cool. You're a nerd."

• • •

"Anthony, are you coming?" asked a lanky teenager.

"What? Oh, hey, Shaun."

"Are you okay? You seem to be in a daze. Welcome back to Earth."

"No kidding. You wouldn't believe the dream I had. Wow, scary, that's all I'll say about it."

"Good, then we can begin this hike we've been planning for months. None of us has ever gone farther than Rocky Ridge and that abandoned coal mine. It's time to see what's on the other side. There's no telling what these woods hold."

77

"Yeah, mountain lions and bears." *Not to mention Urban Carbon Monoxide's old dungeon in the mine*, thought Anthony, falling in line behind Shaun.

"Don't start that again. If you're scared, you can stay home."

"I'm just kidding. Where's everyone else?"

"They're up ahead. I told them to keep going. We'll catch up with them in a minute. Remember, we had to go back for these sandwiches. You have been in a dream world, haven't you?"

"Yeah, but I'm back now, and I feel great. Did you bring your music?"

"Naw, I wanted to rough it like in the old days when they didn't have electronics. But I wish I had my new CD now. Have you heard Mendeleev's new title track, 'P-Orbitals Filling Non-Metals,' from his Periodic Table album?"

"Nope. Isn't that a Russian group?"

"Yeah, I think they're actually from Siberia."

"Cool. I like that group called Boyle's Law and their new song, 'P1 times V1 equals P2 times V2.'"

"They rock! That song reminds me of the Charles' Law old hit, 'V1 divided by V2 equals T1 divided by T2.'"

"Where do they come up with the names for those songs?"

"You got me. They must be running out of names with so many songs out there now."

"True."

The two boys trudged through the heavy undergrowth. Saplings and seedlings raised their small limbs skyward, straining to reach the heights of their aged predecessors. The wind playfully tossed golden brown leaves about the carpet of pine needles. Tree branches swayed rhythmically with the gentle breeze. Beyond a small rise a gurgling stream wound through the maze of standing timber.

Anthony kicked a pine cone. "Hey, my shoe's untied. Keep going, Shaun. I'll meet you on the other side of that small hill. I just need to tie my shoe."

"No problem."

Yanking the laces, Anthony tightened his sneaker. Pulling the string once more, the shoelace snapped, causing his hand to recoil and strike him in the mouth. "Ouch! That'll leave a mark. Only I would wait until we're ten miles into the forest to break my shoestring. This is just great. I'll have to flop around the rest of the way. Hey, Shaun, hold up!"

Favoring his right leg, the one-shoed adolescent skipped up the hill.

"Where'd he go? Shaun, where are you? This isn't funny. You can come out from wherever you're hiding. I broke my shoestring, and I'm not in the mood to play games. I'm serious. I'm going to sit right here until you come out."

Crossing his legs, Anthony plopped on top of the hill. He struggled without success to see through the dense vegetation. A gust of wind whistled through the trees.

"This is ridiculous. Shaun, can you hear me?" he shouted.

Something rustled the branches in the thick shrubbery bordering the left side of the hill's crest. Grinning, Anthony removed his defective shoe and flung it at the hedge. A masked raccoon sprang from the lilac bush and bounded across the startled youth's lap.

"Aaah, you scared me to death!" shouted Anthony, watching the critter disappear into the wilderness. "Shaun must have kept going. He wouldn't wait this long to scare me. He doesn't have the patience to hide forever. Where am I? I don't remember how we got here. I should have paid attention to where we were going instead of blindly following Shaun."

Rising to a standing position, the teen surveyed his surroundings. Nothing looks familiar, he thought. *I'm lost. I can't believe they left me. What's that noise? I'm not waiting here any longer*, thought Anthony, hopping to the bush and retrieving his shoe.

Slipping the sneaker over his foot, he hobbled toward the stream. The water swirled rapidly around the bend in the rivulet. Farther upstream, the current moved less quickly. However, the stream was almost as wide as a river at that point. Anthony watched a distant turtle clinging to a log and basking in the sun. Closer to him, minnows danced in chaotic patterns at the streamlet's bank. A water moccasin wound a course through the rippling current.

"Yikes, I'm not getting in there. I don't know what to do. Shaun!" hollered Anthony, scooping a rock from the ground and flinging it into the stream, scattering the minnows. "I'm thirsty, and you have the water and sandwiches. You should have come back for me by now. Shaun, where are you?"

Panting in short, frantic breaths, he briskly walked along the stream. Perspiration soaked the back of his shirt. The waterway grew wider, spilling into a murky lake.

"Surely, they would have stopped at the lake. It's so quiet. Please, don't leave me out here!" pleaded Anthony. "I'll die! Ollie Oxygen, Xerxes Xenon, where are you? You promised you would come anytime we wore our element glasses. My glasses, where'd I put them? Oh, my...my ring is missing too. What's happening to me? Why am I lost? Someone help me," Anthony cried with tears rolling down his face.

"Calm down," Anthony told himself. "I need to stay calm. Someone will miss me soon, and then they'll look for me. I'll just wait by the lake. Everything will be okay as long as I don't panic. I must be going crazy," he murmured. "I'm even talking to myself. Something is wrong with this picture."

Inhaling the fresh air, he wiped his cheek with the back of his hand. The gentle breeze cooled his flushed face. Mesmerized by the rustling leaves and steady current, his eyes wandered to a rabbit cautiously chomping on a clump of grass.

"It's beautiful out here. It's almost magic," he said. "I don't know why I was worried. I might never have another opportunity to relax and enjoy the wonders of nature in complete silence. It's unbelievable. I don't know why I never saw things this clearly before? Snap out of it. Now I sound like my parents. Get a grip on yourself. Come on, Anthony. Why don't I have any supplies with me? I can't believe I call myself a Boy Scout when their motto is 'Be Prepared.' I'm not prepared for anything, and I'm lost. Some Scout I am. I'll never earn my Eagle at this rate. Why am I worried about becoming an Eagle Scout at a time like this. I'm going nuts. Think, think, think! Gotta stay calm."

"This way," called a voice from across the lake.

"What? Is someone over there? Shaun? Guys?"

"Come on, this way."

"Okay, I'm on my way," Anthony said, perking up. "How do I get across the lake? Wait, wait, look! There's a rock path across the narrow part of the lake. I hope there's no algae on the rocks. That would make them slippery. I wish I had learned to swim better when I was younger. Here goes nothing."

Like a circus acrobat walking a tight rope, Anthony placed one foot in front of the other and stepped from one rock to the next. Steadying himself by holding his arms perpendicular to his body, he made his way to the middle of the lake. A space the length of a yardstick separated him from the next smooth stone. The adolescent cleared his lungs of air and inhaled deeply. Without further hesitation, he stretched his right leg forward as far as possible, barely catching the rock. Straddled between the two stones, he attempted to shift his weight to his forward leg, but his foot twisted out of his untied shoe and he flipped into the water. The current pulled him farther into the lake.

Flailing his arms and kicking wildly, he lunged for the rocks but missed. "Help, I can't swim! Help!" He yelled.

Anthony sucked in a mouth full of water and slipped beneath the murky surface. Kicking, he surged to the top. He coughed and gasped for air. His water-logged shoes and jeans once again dragged him into the lake's mysterious depths. With burning lungs Anthony violently drove his legs upward and clawed desperately at the water. Dizziness clouded his mind. Attempting to inhale, he drew water through his nose, burning his nostrils and throat. He could hear his heart pounding in his ears, and his lungs felt as if they were being torn from his chest.

• • •

"Richard, are you awake?"
"Huh? Yes, who are you?"
"I'm Ashley, your doctor."
"My doctor? Where am I?"
"It's okay. You're in the hospital."
"Why?"
"You were struck by a car while skating."
"I don't remember anything."
"The brain will often block out traumatic events. You've been here for two days slipping in and out of consciousness."

"No wonder I've been in la-la land. I've had the weirdest dreams."

"That happens frequently after an accident such as yours."

"So, when can I go home?"

"We're not sure yet, but soon."

"What's wrong with me? I can't move my arm."

"It's broken."

"Oh, did you immobilize it?

"No, you also suffered a C5, C7 spinal injury."

"What? Is that bad? What are you talking about?"

"You broke your neck. Only time will tell how bad it is. Rest for now."

"Am I paralyzed?"

"It may only be temporary. Because you're young, we were able to use some experimental procedures. I can't promise..."

"No, I'm not handicapped. Help me up."

"Not now, you need your rest. Tomorrow, we'll see about starting your physical therapy. I'm sorry..."

"Get me out of here! I want to walk. I don't want to live in a wheelchair. I'm not a cripple. I want to run!"

"Listen, dear, I know it's tough. But just because you are in a wheelchair doesn't mean the world is over. Use your mind, and you can accomplish anything you want."

"That's easy for you to say. You can get out of bed. You can feed yourself. You can bathe yourself and go to the bathroom. You can hug someone you love. I can't!"

"There are so many things you can do. Listen, I have to leave for a minute, but your family is in the other room."

"Tell them to go away. They can't see me like this. I want to be alone."

"It's your decision. I'll give you some time," said Ashley, disappearing from the patient's bedside.

"Time. That's all I have now. Why? Why didn't I die?" cried Richard, tears welling in his eyes.

Unable to move, he rolled his eyes from side to side scanning from the bed railing to the ceiling and back to the bed railing. He sniffled and stared at the ceiling. Tears blurred his vision. A fly buzzed over his head, eventually settling on his forehead. Instinctively he tried to raise his arm to swat the fly, but nothing moved.

"Get it off me," screamed Richard, sobbing and choking on his saliva.

• • •

"Who turned off the lights?" cried Jeanne-Marie, probing the pitch-blackness with her hands. "Anthony, turn on the light. I'm afraid of the dark. I want Mommy!"

Looking up, Jeanne-Marie watched the moon slip from behind a dark cloud. The unveiled glowing orb illuminated a paved road lined with trees. Having shed their leaves for winter, the branches reached out like fingers attempting to snatch their prey.

"The trees are alive. They're monsters! Mommy, they're going to get me. What's that noise? I can't see."

Bawling fervently, Jeanne-Marie raced along the street, her short legs pumping faster and faster. Losing her balance, the child stumbled and fell forward, sliding to a halt on the rough pavement. She blew on her scratched hands and brushed the dirt from her knees. Huddling into a ball, she sat in the middle of the road, whimpering.

• • •

"They'll bite me," screamed Catherine, watching a line of spiders, roaches, ants, and crickets crawling up her legs.

A dragonfly landed on her nose and stared into her eyes. Flies, bees, and mosquitoes swarmed about her head. Dangling from a thin, silk filament, an Orange Garden Spider rappelled from Catherine's ear to her shoulder. She shivered despite the hot, humid air swirling about her.

She opened her mouth to cry, and a fly, buzzing above her, landed on her tongue. Catherine's face turned green. Spitting and gagging, she shook her head from side to side.

"Help! This can't be real! But I can see them. I hear them buzzing around me. I feel them crawling on my skin. Yuck, I can even smell a stinkbug. And I can...can taste them. How can this not be real? What did my brother say? Oh yeah, they're just bugs. They won't hurt you. There's nothing to be afraid of. Oh, it tickles," giggled Catherine, unclenching her fists and observing where her nails had dug into her hands. "They don't hurt. They're still ugly and gross, but they don't hurt. Hello, Mr. Dragonfly. I must be going crazy. I'm talking to bugs. Hey, they're disappearing. Where are they going?"

The bugs marching up her legs vanished. Those flying about her head darted into the distance. Taking flight, the dragonfly snatched the spider from Catherine's shoulder and flew away. A haze enveloped the small girl.

"Clifton Chlorine, it was you!" yelled Catherine, as she sprang to her feet and confronted the element emerging from the mist.

"You survived," hissed Clifton Chlorine. "The others will not be so fortunate. No matter, you will die anyway."

• • •

"You choked big time," said Adrienne, sweeping her hair behind her ears. "This was your one chance to do something right. You could at least have proved that you were a talented, dare I say, musician. But no, you really blew it!"

"Adrienne, wait. This has to be a mistake. I've never played like this or dressed like this before. My mom wouldn't let me out of the house like this," said Jacqueline, hugging her cello.

"Thank goodness your mom has fashion sense. You're embarrassing me."

"I don't know what's happening now. But I know we were friends in the past."

"Don't say such a thing. She lies."

"Adrienne, you can accuse me of whatever you want. I know the truth, and I will speak the truth. As long as I do what is right, it doesn't matter what others think of me. I will be happy, and my happiness will make others happy even if you choose not to be my friend. We've had some wonderful times in the past, and I will hold onto those memories forever. However, I will now play this piece of music to the best of my ability no matter how awful it sounds. As long as I play the best I can and try my hardest, that's all anyone can ask of me. At least, I'm up here trying and not sitting in the audience making fun of people." said Jacqueline.

"Jacqueline..."

"Yes...Everything's turning fuzzy. Am I going blind? I can't see anything but smoke. Fire!" shouted Jacqueline, diving on the floor.

"Jacqueline, it's me, Catherine! You're okay. Everything you just saw wasn't real. It was Clifton Chlorine's fault."

"Oh, thank you, thank you. That was horrible."

"Not as horrible as your death," hissed Clifton Chlorine. "I'm furious. No one is supposed to survive my dreams of fear."

● ● ●

*I can't breathe. Don't let me die*, thought Anthony, flailing his arms wildly beneath the water's surface. *Relax. That's what my swim instructor said when I was preparing for the swimming merit badge. Relax. I wish I hadn't quit swimming lessons. I have to relax.*

With a series of powerful scissors kicks, Anthony surged to the surface. Spitting and gasping for air, he floated onto his back, spreading his arms and legs open wide. To his astonishment, he did not sink. Instead, he gazed into the sky and breathed heavily.

"Look how cloudy it's getting," he mused.

"There are no clouds in here. Anthony, wake up!" begged Catherine, beating Anthony on the chest. He slid his arms back and forth along the hospital floor as if he was making snow angels.

"Wha...I'm alive. I'm so happy to see you. You'll never believe what happened. It felt so real. But it wasn't real."

"But I am," sneered Clifton Chlorine. "You runts wear my patience thin. Err...even the little girl moves. It will be her last move!"

"Jeanne-Marie, can you hear me?" asked Catherine.

"Mommy, is that you? I'm afraid of the dark. You said nothing would hurt me. I can't see. I believe you, Mommy. I'm brave. The dark can't hurt me. It's just the sun closing his eyes. He'll open them in the morning. I'm okay, Mommy. Don't worry about me," said Jeanne-Marie, rocking to and fro in her huddled, seated position.

"That's right, baby, nothing will harm you. We're right here."

"Catherine, hi," cried Jeanne-Marie, throwing her arms upward and latching onto her sister's neck

"How touching. I think I'm going to be sick," muttered Clifton Chlorine, clenching his fists. "Rejoice in your short existence for five little mice went to sleep, but only four awakened."

"Richard isn't moving," said Anthony, lifting his brother's arm. "His whole body is limp. Even when I pinch him, he doesn't budge. It's as if he's paralyzed or something."

"Good guess, he is paralyzed in his mind. He thinks it's real, and he can't handle it, so, he'll die," cackled Clifton Chlorin.

"No!" shouted Anthony. "Richard, wake up! It's all in your mind. Forget about your body. I know it's not easy, but your mind and spirit are whole. Use them to overcome this. There is so much you can do with a strong mind and spirit. Don't give up. You can beat it!"

"Beat it, stupid fly. Get away from me. Someone help me!" screamed Richard, clamping his eyes shut.

"Richard. Richard, can you hear me?" asked Anthony, shaking his brother by the arm. "We're here for you. All of us, Catherine, Jacqueline, Jeanne-Marie, we're right here. Come back to us. We're waiting for you."

"This is tugging at my heart strings. What a tear jerker, I think I might cry. Wake up, Richard. I'm here for you," mocked Clifton Chlorine, contorting his face into an evil grin.

"His breathing is shallow...his chest is hardly moving. Richard, speak to me!" begged Anthony.

"Ah, yes, it won't be long now. First, the breathing falters, then it stops permanently, leaving one less human sucking up oxygen. Oh, then my favorite part begins when rigor mortis creeps in. That even rhymes a little," chuckled Clifton Chlorine.

"He won't die!" screamed Anthony, leaping to his feet. "I'll teach you a lesson you'll never forget. "By the power of the transition metals, I summon..."

"Anthony, stop! Save your powers. Remember how titanium and chlorine combine to form a smoke screen," warned Catherine, grabbing her brother's outstretched hand. "But, I'll give that monster something to think about. By the power of the alkaline earth metals, I summon beryllium!"

A silvery-gray powder flashed from Catherine's emerald ring. Slamming into Clifton Chlorine, the powder clung to him, dragging him to the ground. Coughing, the enraged element brushed himself with his hands to dislodge the fine particles.

"Do you think this will stop me? It's only a minor inconvenience. I bet you didn't realize beryllium is a very light metal. Look, I can still fly. A little water and acid or electricity will separate me from your dust. It's a wonderful process called electrolysis."

"Richard's breathing better," whispered Anthony. "Keep Clifton Chlorine distracted. It's working!"

Nodding, Catherine further provoked the chlorine element. "You might be able to fly, but you're slower than a chicken waiting for Farmer Brown to take him to the butcher."

"You talk tough, little lady, for someone with so little time left. I am chlorine..."

"No, you're not," said Catherine. "You're beryllium chloride, a combination of beryllium and chlorine. In fact, beryllium's mighty valence bonding has a strong attraction for your electrons. You won't find enough water or electricity here to separate you from my beryllium no matter how badly you want to perform electrolysis. I'm smarter than you give me credit for. You don't know what other tricks I have up my sleeve. No one is afraid of you."

"Don't toy with me, child," said Clifton Chlorine. "I will make this world scarier than your dreams, worse even than death."

"Just a little longer," whispered Anthony. "His eyes flickered."

"Go away, fly. I can still do some things for myself," said Richard, extending his lower jaw beyond his upper lip and blowing air across his forehead.

"Richard!"

"Hey, Anthony. Don't feel sorry for me because I'm paralyzed. I'm still human and I can do anything I put my mind to..."

"It was a dream! Look, you can move your arms."

"I...I can. I'm not paralyzed! I promise to thank God every day for letting me walk," said Richard, tears streaming down his cheeks like flood waters through a city street.

"What, he lives?" asked Clifton Chlorine. "Although somewhat entertaining, this has been a spoiled moment of satisfaction. Nonetheless, you're still helpless. And your time in this world has expired."

# CHAPTER ELEVEN
## Episode Eleven
# "Tabitha Tantalum"

"You are the one whose time has expired. And I thought I spoke too much. I have never heard such mindless chatter. It's giving me a headache," muttered Xerxes Xenon.

"Well, I wouldn't want to annoy his highness," retorted Clifton Chlorine. "I can't believe I'm in the presence of a noble gas. Should I bow? No, who would humble themselves to such a windbag as you. Instead, I'll put a quick end to your miserable, snobbish existence, too!" he threatened, with a growl.

"It is your move, Clifton Chlorine. I will not argue with you and your idle threats," replied Xerxes Xenon. "Surrender would be advisable. You can no longer hide behind your smoke screen. You knew the smoke would eventually dissipate. Oh, I apologize for using such an advanced vocabulary word as 'dissipate.' Let me rephrase that to allow your simple mind to better comprehend what I am saying. Uh-hum, you knew that the smoke would thin to the point of invisibility. You simply did not expect us to be here when it did...with nowhere to hide, you will face the consequences of your crimes," he said, pointing accusingly at the suspect element.

"Idle threats, consequences of my crimes, you are full of accusations," Clifton Chlorine said with contempt. "You think that you are the king of the elements. Sir Xerxes Xenon, what a joke! You are so full of yourself that you think everyone has forgotten your weaknesses. Well, I haven't. Do you recall the London dispersion forces? Ah, I see the fear in your eyes. Your weakness even holds the name of your home, London.

In fact, isn't that where humans first discovered you and your pathetic kingdom? No matter, let me share your weakness with those among us. Hey, kids, when Xerxes Xenon attempts to blast me with his so-called blinding ray, I will smash it because of the London dispersion forces existing between his xenon atoms. You see, at times even his electrons fall out of symmetrical order in their subatomic shells, causing weak forces between his noble gas atoms. These weak forces are called 'London dispersion forces.' Not only will the existence of London dispersion forces allow me to convert Xerxes Xenon's gas into a solid; but since Xerxes Xenon's atom is so heavy, London dispersion forces are a more common occurrence. In other words, the importance of London dispersion forces greatly increases as the size of the atom increases. And Xerxes Xenon, you are one big atom in comparison to the other atoms here. What have you got to say now? I've never before seen the great Xerxes Xenon at a loss for words. Oh well, you shall face your destruction in silence. I will punish you."

"I will execute the punishment," seethed a voice from behind the children and elements. "Everyone is guilty. Everyone dies!"

Spinning around, the stunned crew stared into Ozzie Ozone's creased pox-marked face. Green toxic gas escaped through his decay-marred nostrils. Raising his arms, the ozone molecule's frayed burlap sleeves slid down to reveal gnarled, burnt hands.

"Ozzie Ozone, don't you dare hurt them!" ordered a wee voice from the dark shadow cast by the ominous molecule.

Flattening herself against the wall, Catherine blinked her eyes, not sure she believed what she saw. She watched Ozzie Ozone in amazement as his menacing scowl melted. Like a feeble old man, the bewildered molecule turned to confront the tiny voice.

No matter how much Catherine craned her neck left and right, she could not see around the molecule's tattered cloak. With an effort, she put aside her curiosity, remembering the trouble it had caused her in the past, and wrapped her arms around Jeanne-Marie. "Oh, Ozzie, poor Ozzie Ozone. It is true. I wish I had found you sooner," said the small voice.

"Tabitha Tantalum, what are you doing here?" asked Ozzie Ozone. "Don't look at me. You can't see me like this. They have turned me into a monster."

"You're no monster. It has been too many years since I last saw you. I heard about your tragedy, but you have been impossible to find," replied Tabitha Tantalum in her quiet voice.

"I wish you had never found me. Please, leave me alone. I don't want anyone to see me. Let me take care of this problem."

"Ozzie Ozone, you can't continue this hateful rampage," said Tabitha Tantalum. "Anger and revenge are not the solution to anything. It is destroying you. Look around you. You can't even see who is trying to help you. Not everyone is here to hurt you."

"Then who is doing it? Who caused the damage to my ozone layer?" asked Ozzie Ozone with building rage. "It was those beasts called humans with their aerosol cans spraying fluorocarbons into the atmosphere. I am trying to protect their fragile world from the sun's harmful ultraviolet rays, and they try to destroy me. I can play their game, too. If they want to die, then I'll introduce them to lethal doses of smog. I'll crush them before the sun ever has a chance to fry their miserable hides. And anyone who stands in my way will die with them!"

"There's that anger again," said Tabitha Tantalum. "It blocks all rational thought so your mind is clouded with rage. If you would stop to think, you'd remember that the United States federal government banned fluorocarbon aerosols in late nineteen-seventy-eight. Also, Freon is slowly being phased out as the chief coolant for air-conditioners. In fact, all over the world humans are making efforts to reduce pollution. Even in refineries, chemical plants are using improved wet-gas scrubbers that can remove over twelve hundred tons of particulate matter per day. In addition, chemists and other scientists continue to develop cleaner alternate fuel sources such as liquefied natural gas and solar energy. Granted, they could do a much better job, but they are at least making an effort. Never mind the humans. We all know the environment can withstand a certain level of pollution. This is evident because forest fires produce more pollution than chemical plants, and forest fires existed for thousands of years before refineries came along. Humans are not your enemy. You only have one true enemy."

"Who? I'll pulverize him."

"That anger is what has caused you to become your true enemy's puppet," Tabitha Tantalum reasoned in her soothing voice. "Your destructive rage has fit perfectly into his plans. With pain-staking precision, he is destroying you while you help him to demolish the world."

"Who is he?"

"He is the one who has combined with these pollutants to form such cancerous compounds as $ClO$, or should I say chlorine-monoxide?"

"Clifton Chlorine!" roared Ozzie Ozone, whirling around, his bedraggled cloak brushing both sides of the hallway.

Catherine and her sisters stumbled backward. Richard and Anthony froze, staring into Ozzie Ozone's creased face. Looking over her shoulder, Catherine searched the hall for Clifton Chlorine.

"Where are you? I will find you. Face me, you coward," snarled Ozzie Ozone, scanning the hall before returning his attention to Tabitha Tantalum. "Why is he doing this to me?"

"Clifton Chlorine is poison. He wants to be the most powerful element in the universe, but you stand in his way. People are discovering that ozone is a safer and more effective bleaching agent, disinfectant, and air purifier than chlorine. Ozone is gradually replacing chlorine as the premier cleaning agent. Clifton Chlorine would never allow that. Once he has finished turning your anger against his enemies, he is planning to destroy you."

"That will never happen. He will pay for the pain he has caused me," seethed Ozzie Ozone. "He will suffer for disfiguring me and transforming me into this hideous monster. Do not try to follow me. This is my fight!" Ozone lumbered past the stunned children and disappeared into the morgue.

Catherine studied Tabitha Tantalum's features: her soft facial features, creating a natural beauty; her eyes, melting the hardest heart and delving into one's deepest emotions; her gray complexion, emanating unusual warmth; and her simple, yet elegant garb, ornamented with the letters "Ta," defining her openly honest, yet complex personality. Holding her breath, Catherine averted her eyes fearing Tabitha Tantalum could read her innermost thoughts. Nevertheless, she could not avoid engaging Tabitha Tantalum's warm gaze, which wrapped her in a sense of security and confidence.

"You have nothing to fear from Ozzie Ozone," assured Tabitha Tantalum, smiling. "His heart, although hardened by decades of abuse, remains gentle and caring beneath it all. Ozone has always tried to help the earth. In fact, you have seen Ozzie Ozone at work more often than you realize. Every lightning flash converts some oxygen into ozone, which then helps to clean the air. Anyway, Ozzie Ozone simply needs some time to himself to sort through everything. We must stop Clifton Chlorine before Ozzie Ozone discovers him and destroys him. As much as everyone dislikes Clifton Chlorine and his baneful behavior, we have to keep him alive, too. He is the only one who can unlock the good secrets of chlorine as well as the evil ones, which he has chosen to use. A little time in Molecule Prison will direct him to the proper path that the element guardians are committed to follow. He will learn the truth and will suffer the consequences of his actions."

"Where's your twin sister, N'bia Niobium?" asked Xerxes Xenon, strutting to the front of the group. Without waiting for an answer, Xerxes Xenon continued, "I suppose N'bia Niobium is in the next room." He turned to the group. "N'bia Niobium and Tabitha Tantalum are rare metals who are always found together in the mineral tantalite." Turning back to Tabitha Tantalum he asked, "By the way, what are you doing here?"

"I was waiting for you to tell me," answered Tabitha Tantalum, smiling. "Actually, I'm here to inspect some of the surgical instruments and implants made from tantalum. But it seems that we have more pressing matters at hand with Clifton Chlorine running rampant in the hospital."

Whispering to Catherine and her siblings, Xerxes Xenon made sure that only the children could hear him. "Don't worry about those London dispersion forces. It is a natural occurrence in both noble gases and nonpolar molecules. There is nothing wrong with having these weak forces between the electrons in my atoms because they actually help me when I make physical changes from a gas to a liquid to a solid. I know when my electrons lose their symmetrical arrangement and temporarily produce a dipolar arrangement of charge. This situation only lasts for a very short time, and it does not hinder my abilities. Clifton Chlorine thought he knew more than he really did."

Catherine attempted to respond but was not sure she understood everything Xerxes Xenon had just said. She presumed he was attempting to protect his pride. In fact, his face was still flushed from the earlier confrontation.

"I have a question," said Ollie Oxygen, snapping Catherine back from her thoughts. "What are Catherine and her brothers and sisters doing on this floor? I thought you were with your parents. I was about to ask Anthony that question when Catherine and Richard stumbled out of the morgue with Clifton Chlorine hot on their heels."

The five siblings hung their heads and stared at the floor. Catherine outlined circles on the floor with the toe of her shoe. Jacqueline nudged Richard with her elbow.

"I apologize for lying," answered Richard, sheepishly. "There's no excuse for us to lie, but we were following Dr. James. We thought you would tell us not to because it would be too dangerous. So we foolishly followed the doctor and almost got killed in our dreams. Actually, we need to get out of here because Dr. James could come back any minute now. I thought..."

Dr. James' wiry frame slipped into the hall. He glared at the children through narrowed, beady eyes. Perspiration trickled down his furrowed brow. He was no longer carrying the Styrofoam cooler.

# CHAPTER TWELVE
## Episode Eleven
# "The Goods"

"What are you kids doing here?" growled Dr. James, pushing through the trembling fivesome. "Do you know what time it is? I remember you three from earlier," he said, looking at the girls. "Parents no longer discipline their kids properly. Otherwise, I wouldn't have to keep running across your snotty-nosed faces. If I catch you brats roaming the halls again, you will feel the sting of true discipline. A little chastisement might do you kids some good. Now get out of here! This is a staff only area. If I wasn't so busy, I'd whip your rear-end right now."

Dr. James stomped to the morgue doors. Pausing at the entrance, the doctor snapped his head around and eyed the children. The five siblings cringed and cowered against the wall.

"And take off those stupid sunglasses. This is a hospital, not the beach," hissed Dr. James, disappearing into the morgue.

"Richard, Anthony, girls, come this way," said Tabitha Tantalum, drifting down the side hall.

The group scurried from the morgue and huddled in the adjoining hallway. Anthony mopped his brow with the tail of his shirt. Catherine released several short breaths and shivered.

"That guy gives me the creeps," muttered Catherine, glancing over her shoulder, fearing Dr. James would step around the corner.

"He is a creep," responded Tabitha Tantalum. "And we need to do something about him."

"We can't forget about Clifton Chlorine either," said Ollie Oxygen, standing beside Tabitha Tantalum. We'll have to divide into two groups to go after each of those villains."

"I concur," spouted Xerxes Xenon. "There is not enough time for us all to chase both those scoundrels. Clifton Chlorine will wreak havoc on this hospital if we fail to locate him, and Dr. James will get away with murder if we give him time to dispose of the evidence. Therefore, Tabitha Tantalum, Richard, and Jacqueline will follow me in the pursuit of Dr. James. Ollie Oxygen will lead the rest of you in the hunt for Clifton Chlorine. I know this sounds barbaric and uncivilized, but we have no other options. I wish there was a more noble procedure for conducting matters, but even the royalty must dirty their hands at some point."

"Well, Sir Xenon took charge of the situation, but it sounds good to me. Let's do it," said Tabitha Tantalum, nodding to Ollie Oxygen, who floated down the hallway.

"I hate splitting up," mumbled Catherine, wiping her sweaty palms against her legs. "Every time we separate, something awful happens."

"We're guardians now. We have no other choice," whispered Anthony. "Come on, Ollie Oxygen is leaving."

"Bye, see you later," said Catherine, waving to her brother and sister.

Waving in return, Jacqueline and Richard watched Catherine, Anthony, and Jeanne-Marie until they rounded the corner and disappeared from sight. Jacqueline pushed her glasses snugly into place on her nose and clutched her brother's hand. Turning their attention to the two elements, the siblings waited for directions.

"What was that noise?" asked Richard, his eyes growing wide.

"It's the morgue doors," answered Tabitha Tantalum. "Quick, get into the stairwell."

The group frantically scurried down the hall and yanked open the door to the stairs. Collapsing on the bottom step, Jacqueline watched her brother creep to the door and slowly rise until he could peek through the window. Xerxes Xenon and Tabitha Tantalum hovered in front of the window. Soon the familiar squeak of gurney wheels echoed through the hall. The chattering wheels grew louder and louder until it sounded as if the cart was coming through the door.

"It's Dr. James," whispered Richard, dropping to his knees. "I don't think he saw me."

"No, he didn't even stop," said Tabitha Tantalum. "He made a left turn. That's the corridor leading to the hospital's basement exit. We have to follow him."

Taking a deep breath, Richard spoke, "Okay, I've read all about shadowing somebody. We can't get too close. My heart is about to jump out of my chest."

"We're right here with you. Everything will be okay," assured Tabitha Tantalum, slipping under the door and joining Xerxes Xenon in the hall.

Grabbing Jacqueline's hand, Richard opened the door and stepped into the corridor. Scooting along the passageway, brother and sister clung to the wall. Richard paused at the end of the hallway, waiting for the elements' next move.

"This way. Hurry, the doctor has left the building," urged Xerxes Xenon, rapidly signaling with his small hand.

The foursome bolted through the corridor skidding to a halt beneath the exit sign hanging over the windowless metal doors. Taking measured steps Richard tiptoed to the door and pressed his ear against the cold metal. Tabitha Tantalum held up her finger and disappeared under the door.

"I don't hear anything," whispered Richard, stepping away from the door and rubbing his ear.

"Maybe he stopped on the other side of the door. I'm scared," whimpered Jacqueline, cowering against the wall.

Before Richard could respond, Tabitha Tantalum reappeared from under the door. Brushing the sleeve of her cloak, she nodded to Xerxes Xenon. Xerxes Xenon nodded and slipped under the door.

"Dr. James is placing everything in a medical van at the end of the loading dock. There's a stack of wooden crates that will keep him from seeing us. Now is our chance to get close enough to see what he is stealing. Xerxes Xenon is keeping watch on the other side."

Without a word, Richard gently pressed the door handle until it clicked. Inhaling sharply, he gently swung the door open. The hinges were well oiled and remained silent. Motioning for Jacqueline to go ahead of him, Richard stepped into the steamy night air and softly shut the door. Both children crouched and duck-walked the short distance from the doors to the stacks of wooden pallets.

In the distance, Dr. James shoved the now-empty gurney away from the van and slammed the rear doors. He adjusted his wire-rimmed spectacles and scanned the loading dock. Yanking a set of keys out of the van's door lock, Dr. James dropped the keys into his lab-coat pocket and pushed the gurney up an incline. When he reached the top of the concrete loading dock, he stopped, straightened, and massaged his lower back.

"Is he coming this way?" whispered Jacqueline.

Richard answered, "I think so."

"I don't think he'll notice you behind these crates," said Tabitha Tantalum, standing atop the highest stack of palettes.

"I'm glad you're so confident since he can't see you without these element glasses," whispered Richard, wiping the sweat from his upper lip.

Once again, the doctor hunched over the gurney and pushed it toward the siblings' hideout. The squeaking wheels drew ever closer. Without pausing, Dr. James walked past the two children and entered the hospital through the heavy metal doors.

"It won't take him long to put that cart back. If we're going to check out the van, we'd better do it now," suggested Richard, standing.

"Yeah, let's get this over with," agreed Jacqueline. "I'm so nervous my stomach hurts."

"Good idea. We'll get whatever evidence we can," said Tabitha Tantalum, streaking toward the van. "Dr. James will probably be inside for a while. I'm sure he'll want to clean the gurney and replace everything exactly as it was. The last thing he wants to do is leave behind any evidence."

Reassured by Tabitha Tantalum's comments, Richard and Jacqueline raced along the loading dock and down the incline. Arriving at the van, Richard grabbed the rear door handle. Jacqueline nervously watched the doors leading into the hospital.

"It's unlocked," gasped Richard, jerking open the door. "Quickly, get inside."

Jacqueline clambered into the van. The two element guardians darted in front of Richard, who entered the van last. Pulling the door closed behind him, the teenager slumped against the van's inner wall.

The loading dock's security lights cast an eerie glow throughout the vehicle's interior. In the dim light, Richard noted a wire-mesh barrier separating the front seats from the rear compartment where he sat. Dropping his right arm, he bumped a rough object.

"The Styrofoam cooler," murmured Richard, under his breath.

"Eek!" screamed Jacqueline, catapulting herself into her brother's lap.

"What's wrong?"

"It...it's...it's a...," stammered Jacqueline, unable to complete her sentence.

Nudging his sister to the side, Richard crawled to the opposite side of the van. Looking down, he stared at a long black plastic bag. The young teen gasped as he contemplated the lumps in the bag.

"It's a body bag," stated Xerxes Xenon. "It contains the remains of Jim, the man Dr. James shot in his office. His corpse is a crucial piece of evidence if we wish to indict the doctor."

"Xerxes Xenon, don't be so crude! The way you said that made it sound awful," exclaimed Tabitha Tantalum. "You are so cold!"

"Well, it is awful. This is reality. There is no way to, as some would say, sugar-coat the truth."

"What are we going to do?" asked Richard, retreating from the bag. "We've got the body, but we still don't have the goods, or whatever Dr. James and Jim called them."

"Yes, we do."

"We do? Where?"

"In the Styrofoam cooler," answered Xerxes Xenon, pointing his glowing finger at the container.

"What did Jim want with a cooler?" asked Jacqueline, regaining her composure.

"It's not the cooler. It's what's inside the cooler," answered Tabitha Tantalum.

"Let's grab it and get out of here. It gives me shivers being this close to a dead guy."

"He will not hurt you. The man you should fear the most is the living one, Dr. James," said Xerxes Xenon. "Somehow we need to remove these items from the van."

"I'm not touching the body bag," exclaimed Jacqueline. She attempted to stand, but banged her head on the van's roof. "That hurt. Let's get out of here."

"Wait, I have to see what's in the cooler," said Richard, unlatching and lifting the lid.

"No! Stop! It's best if you don't know..."

"Gross," blurted Richard, dropping the lid. "What is it?"

"Human organs, specifically, Jim's heart, lungs, liver, and kidneys. Replace the cover. The organs must be kept cold, or they are of no use to anyone," instructed Xerxes Xenon, shaking his head.

Covering his mouth with his left hand, Richard clutched the lid with his trembling right hand and fit it snugly on top of the open container. Before Jacqueline could express her disgust, the "click" of a lock was heard. Spinning around, the frightened twosome stared through the window into Dr. James' gaunt face. Surveying the ground around the van, the doctor appeared oblivious to the presence of his stowaways. Not even taking a moment to peer through the van's rear windows, Dr. James removed the key he had just used in the van's door lock and walked out of sight.

The stunned children heard footsteps crunching along the side of the van to the front of the vehicle. Squeaking hinges announced the opening of the driver's door. The van rocked gently as the doctor entered the van and slammed the door. The vinyl seat creaked from Dr. James' weight. Within seconds the van roared to life.

"Help!" mouthed Jacqueline, crying softly.

Lurching forward, the van's acceleration tossed Jacqueline and Richard against the rear doors. The garbled sounds of a radio talk show drifted from the front muffling the children's crash against the cold metal. Holding his sister, Richard clung to the door's hinges to keep from sliding.

"This isn't good," uttered Tabitha Tantalum.

"That is apparent," grumbled Xerxes Xenon. "Why don't we think of something slightly more productive than the obvious situation into which we have stumbled, like a solution that gets us out of this crude source of transportation? No noble should be carted around in such a homely piece of metal like some common laborer. I will bet this vehicle does not even have decent shocks. I can feel every bump," he complained as he rose from sitting beside the Styrofoam container. He gently rubbed his backside.

"We get the point, Xerxes Xenon. What did you have in mind?"

"A simple distraction. I will blind the doctor with a xenon blast and Jacqueline can unleash some fireworks. In the confusion, Dr. James will lose control of the vehicle and crash. Then we can escape. It is almost the way that Richard and Anthony escaped Rhodes when the earthquake toppled Colossus."

"Have all these bumps we've been hitting jostled your brain loose?" said Tabitha Tantalum, shaking her head. "We can't crash the van. Richard and Jacqueline would be injured or killed. They're humans, not elements. Besides, the door is locked, and there's a wire mesh separating us from the front of the van. We wouldn't be able to escape even if the van was stopped and the doctor had disappeared."

Richard suddenly stared at Xerxes Xenon through wide-open eyes. Excitement flushed his face. Pointing at the frames of his glasses, Richard frantically moved his finger back and forth.

"I wish it was that simple," said Xerxes Xenon, acknowledging Richard's wild gesturing. "I realize we used the bumps along the frames of your glasses to create a portal to ancient Greece and to the Great One's kingdom, but remember, every location on earth creates an opening to a different world and time. If we created a portal, we would all land in different places because the van is moving. Thus, every couple of meters the van moves, the portal changes. Second, even if the vehicle was not moving, the portal could lead to someplace more dangerous than this van or could leave us trapped in a world from which we could not return for weeks, years, or centuries. It is too dangerous. Believe it or not, we are safer here."

The color drained from Richard's face. Slumping his shoulders, he dropped his head and gazed at the floor. Jacqueline tightly squeezed her brother's arm and wiped the tears trickling down her cheeks.

The vehicle careened around a corner and bounced to an abrupt stop, flinging Richard and Jacqueline against the wire mesh. Dr. James pushed open the door and sprung from the truck. The sound of jingling keys heralded the doctor's arrival at the van's rear doors.

# "Bad Gas"

"This way!" yelled Catherine. She raced up the stairs and flung open the door. "I don't see Clifton Chlorine anywhere."

"This isn't hide and seek. We could die if we run into Clifton Chlorine. Slow down," scolded Anthony, holding the door for Jeanne-Marie. "I don't want to have any more nightmares."

"Anthony's right. Clifton Chlorine will be waiting for us..."

"Mama!" squealed Jeanne-Marie, waddling down the hall as fast as her little legs could carry her.

"There you are. Where have you been?" asked the children's mother, scooping Jeanne-Marie off the ground. "Where are Richard and Jacqueline?"

"Uh, they should be here any minute now," answered Catherine, nervously twisting her hair around her finger. "We'll go get them."

"No, you won't. I don't want you kids running around the hospital. Sit over here on the bench," ordered Catherine's mother, placing Jeanne-Marie on the bench against the wall.

"I forgot about your mom," said Ollie Oxygen, resting on one of the thin branches extending from the leafy potted plant beside the furniture.

"Why do you kids always wear those sunglasses? We're inside the hospital and it's dark outside."

"Uh, yeah, I forgot I had them on," responded Anthony, following his siblings in removing his glasses.

"That's better. Is anyone else thirsty? I'm going to get a drink from the water fountain."

"No, thank you," answered Catherine, slumping against the blue wall.

The children's mother walked to the water fountain across the hall. Stooping, she held her hair in a pony-tail and sipped from the fountain. Dropping her hair, she clutched the edge of the fountain with both hands and swayed shakily from side to side. The children's mother shook her head and attempted to stand up straight; but her knees buckled, and she collapsed to the floor.

"Mommy!" cried Jeanne-Marie, hopping off the bench and racing to her mother.

"This happened to people on the third and fourth floors, too," exclaimed Nurse Amy, sprinting to the children's fallen mother. She called for help.

"Clifton Chlorine," muttered Anthony, through clenched teeth.

"She'll be okay, sweetie," assured Amy, hugging Jeanne-Marie. "These men will take her to a room where she can rest until she feels better."

Two orderlies arrived in response to the nurse's summons and lifted Jeanne-Marie's mother onto a gurney and wheeled her down the hall. Amy held Jeanne-Marie's hand. Holding a flood of tears at bay, Catherine joined Anthony next to Amy.

"Come with me to the lounge," said Amy, directing the threesome through a series of doors. "You'll be safe here, and I'll be back in a little while to take you to see your mom when she awakens. Are you okay?"

"We're okay," answered Anthony. "I'll watch my sisters."

"Where's your other brother and sister?"

"Oh, somewhere near, they'll be here any minute. I'll let them know what happened."

"Great, I'll be back," promised Amy, waving and departing the room through the rear door.

Standing silently in the middle of the empty lounge, Catherine observed the rows of flower-covered furniture. A few tables, a desk, and a pay phone completed the room's furnishings. Catherine gently patted her sister's shoulder and peered questioningly at her brother.

"We can't sit here and do nothing. Clifton Chlorine will probably be hunting for us. Let's see what the elements think we should do," suggested Anthony, slipping on his sunglasses.

"Hey, we've got to go. Caspar Calcium has Clifton Chlorine cornered," exclaimed Ollie Oxygen, hovering above the children.

"Are you serious?"

"Scouts honor! Yes, this way. Don't worry about your mom. She will recover quickly."

Anthony and his sisters clambered into the hallway to follow Ollie Oxygen. Scampering nonchalantly past hospital employees, the sunglass-clad children weaved through a maze of corridors and down a flight of stairs. Entering a room marked "Employees Only," Anthony gazed at his sisters. The girls nervously surveyed their surroundings. They were unable to clearly distinguish any objects in the dark.

"Isn't this the room next to the morgue?" whispered Catherine, mirroring her brothers nervous expression.

"I don't know. I wish we could fry Clifton Chlorine and not have to come near here again," grumbled Anthony.

"Fry, that's a strange way to phrase it. I'd like to punish him severely," said Catherine, in a hushed tone.

"I'm afraid we can't hurt Clifton Chlorine," remarked Ollie Oxygen, pausing in the center of the room.

"I know, I know. Clifton Chlorine helps us," replied Catherine. "We even learned in school how more than eleven million tons of chlorine are produced in the United States each year and..."

"That's right! Chlorine is by far the most commercially important element of the halogen family. Unfortunately, he is in the same family as Io Iodine and, like Io, is diatomic, as you saw at the pool when he transformed into the diatomic molecule $Cl_2$. No matter how evil he may be in some areas, chlorine is still helpfully used as a bleach in the paper and textile industries and in PVC plastic production."

"Ollie Oxygen, you sound like Xerxes Xenon," giggled Jeanne-Marie.

"Sorry, I got carried away. By now I should realize you know the importance of each element, no matter how unusual or rare it may be. Come on, let's get Clifton Chlorine before he causes any more trouble."

The small group stumbled through the dark room. Arriving at a door on the far side of the room, Ollie Oxygen placed his index finger on his lips and motioned for Anthony to open the door. The adjoining room's bright lights blinded their eyes.

"Stay back!" warned Caspar Calcium. "I can't contain Clifton Chlorine much longer." The weary element blasted another silvery ray into Clifton Chlorine, who calmly smirked at his opponent and returned fire.

"What's all that powder?" asked Jeanne-Marie, peeking from behind her brother's leg.

"It's the molecule calcium chloride. When a calcium element connects with two chlorine atoms, it forms the compound calcium chloride, which is used as a drying agent," answered Ollie Oxygen, yelling above the hissing rays as they exploded into each other. "Unfortunately, it takes..."

"Aaah," screamed Caspar Calcium, spinning from Clifton Chlorine's yellow blast and crashing to the floor.

Caspar Calcium attempted to stand, but his legs buckled, and he fell to his knees. Stretching his right hand forward, he grasped his spear. Using it like a cane, Caspar Calcium struggled to his feet. Clifton Chlorine hurled a yellow-green flurry of chlorine at Caspar Calcium, knocking Caspar Calcium's spear from his hand and smashing the exhausted element against the wall. The small spear clattered to the floor, and Caspar Calcium slid down the wall, folding into a crumpled ball on the floor.

"I won't even waste your time explaining the hideous death you will suffer from my suffocating fumes!" seethed Clifton Chlorine, unleashing a cloud of yellow gas.

Grasping his sister by the arm, Anthony pulled Jeanne-Marie into the room. Ollie Oxygen darted through the haze shielding Caspar Calcium from another blast from Clifton Chlorine. The wounded element struggled to raise himself once again from the floor, but his trembling body buckled and collapsed.

"Caspar Calcium, get up!" screamed Catherine, choking from the poisonous gas. She staggered through an open door into the laboratory.

"Stop!" ordered Dr. Kalium, marching into the frenzied midst. "By the power of the active metals, I summon potassium!"

"No, get away from me!" squealed Clifton Chlorine, desperately dodging the white streaks exploding from Dr. Kalium's outstretched palms.

113

"Clifton Chlorine, you are a spoiled juvenile. It should be an honor to be the guardian of such a widely used element as chlorine. But you would rather wreak havoc throughout the element world, especially when something does not go your way. You almost went too far in attacking Ozzie Ozone. That could have caused your death. A little time in juvenile detention at Molecule Prison should give you time to ponder the errors of your actions," lectured Dr. Kalium, stepping closer to Clifton Chlorine.

"You...you can't make me go," cried Clifton Chlorine, struggling to break the streaks encircling him like a python strangling its prey.

"I am ashamed of your behavior, and even now you fight the laws of the chemical world," said Dr. Kalium, shaking his head and watching the streaks form rope-like cords binding Clifton Chlorine's arms to his sides. "There is no way to prevent my positive ions from combining with your negative ions to form the stable, neutral white solid known as potassium chloride. That stability will keep you from forming any other compounds."

"And in case you think about jumping into water to separate the positive and negative ions, I'll add a little oxygen," exclaimed Ollie Oxygen, blasting Clifton Chlorine with blue rays. "It will take more than water to free you from the molecule potassium chlorate, which we have created by joining potassium and oxygen to your chlorine. That should hold until we arrive at Molecule..."

"Prison is the least of his worries," cackled Ozzie Ozone, creeping into the hall. "I will handle matters from here."

114

# CHAPTER FOURTEEN
## Episode Eleven
# "Caught"

"Where is the lousy key?" snarled Dr. James, his voice rattling the inside of the van.

"Where can we hide?" whispered Jacqueline, clutching her brother's arm.

"Stay behind me. I'll think of something," answered Richard. His teeth chattered and he nervously anticipated the van door opening. The children quietly listened to the keys rattling together.

The jingling stopped. Then, the sound of the key scraping against the inner workings of the lock broke the silence. Jacqueline clamped her hands over her ears but could not mute the metallic click of the lock releasing its grip. Richard whipped his arm in front of him, holding his Ring of Enlightenment before him. The door flew open.

"By the power of the transition elements, I summon chromium!" yelled Richard.

"What the...?" began Dr. James, before being splattered by the coat of red paint exploding from Richard's ring. "My eyes, I can't see!" he shouted.

"Run, Jacqueline, get out of the van!" yelled Richard, yanking the keys from the door lock. "Jacqueline, catch," said Richard, tossing the keys to his sister. "We'll..."

A rapidly approaching sedan spotlighted the siblings with its blinding high beams. The kids stood frozen, watching the car screech to a halt within inches of them. Two men sprang from the vehicle and sprinted toward them, the roadside gravel crunching under their heavy boots.

"Dr. Ray," sputtered Richard. "I thought you were still at the hospital."

"Never mind us, what are you two doing out here?" asked Dr. Ray, holding out his arm to prevent his companion from drawing any closer to Richard and Jacqueline.

"Meddlesome kids, I knew you were nothing but trouble," grumbled Dr. James, clasping his paint-smeared spectacles in his left hand. "Little girl, hand over the keys. I'll only ask once."

"Dr. Ray, help us," pleaded Richard. "Dr. James has a cooler full of organs and a dead body in the van. He's a murderer."

"What a harsh accusation for one so young to be making," Dr. James said. "I'm afraid it's true, though. Unfortunately, Dr. Ray is as guilty in this matter as I might be..."

"I didn't murder anyone," snipped Dr. Ray, glaring at Dr. James through narrowed eyes.

"A bit touchy are we? Alas, that may be true, yet I see we don't mind profiting from such a murder. Nevertheless, we have our deal, Dr. Ray. You will mind your manners and remember your place," snarled Dr. James, snatching a revolver from under his cloak. "Now, I want to see some keys, or there will be a few more dead bodies."

"No, stay away from her!" yelled Richard, holding his ring before the doctor.

"Quiet, boy," growled Dr. James as he pistol whipped Richard across the back of the skull with the firearm's handgrip.

Searing pain ripped through Richard's brain. Spots flashed before his eyes. Then all went black. With a grunt, the boy collapsed in a clump of grass jutting into the roadside gravel.

"Richard..."

"The keys, Child," ordered Dr. James, stepping over Richard's body.

"Never!" screamed Jacqueline, running past Dr. Ray.

"I've got her," yelled Dr. Ray's companion, cutting off Jacqueline's escape route.

With Dr. James and the other assailant encircling her, Jacqueline backed away, keeping an eye on both men. Taking another step, she bumped into a steel guardrail. The young girl glanced over her shoulder and peered into a deep ravine choked with thick vegetation.

"If you want them, go get them," yelled Jacqueline, flinging the keys with all her strength.

"No!" roared Dr. James, watching the keys disappear into the darkness.

Two burly hands snatched Jacqueline, lifting her off the ground. The man slung the girl over his shoulder like a sack of potatoes and ambled toward the sedan. Dr. James remained near the railing, tightly clenching his jaw muscles.

"Put the imp and her brother in the trunk," ordered the infuriated doctor.

"You don't have to do that. I'll watch them," replied Dr. Ray, taking Jacqueline from the other man.

"Fool, you can't watch them!" snarled Dr. James. "We have to dispose of the body, and then we'll have to get rid of the rug rats, too. Now put her in the trunk."

"Why, Dr. Ray, why are you helping him?" cried Jacqueline, wiping her tears on her shirt.

"I have no choice. Years ago, my father needed a heart transplant, and we were running out of time. They couldn't find one anywhere. I had just graduated from medical school and had begun working at the hospital as an intern under the twisted, demented Dr. James. He told me he could get a heart. Unfortunately, it cost more than I could pay, and no one would give me a loan for the money since I couldn't tell them what the money was for. You see, I couldn't tell anyone where the heart was coming from because it was from the black market where they sell stolen organs. So Dr. James gave me the heart under the condition that I would work for him and his illegal operation until my debt was paid."

"You're breaking my heart," sneered Dr. James, rolling his eyes. "Save your sad story for someone who cares. I've heard more than I can tolerate. Oh, your poor daddy."

"I won't let you hurt these kids. I've done everything you've asked but I have to draw the line here."

"I don't have time to argue with you. Imbeciles surround me! Gary, put the kids in the trunk."

"Yes, sir," answered the large man. "Dr. Ray, let me have her. You know what's at stake here. If we get caught, we could spend the rest of our lives behind bars."

Shaking his head and gazing at the ground, Dr. Ray reluctantly released his hold on Jacqueline. Gary once again lifted the small girl like a bag of rice and also scooped Richard off the ground. With one child draped over his shoulder and the other tucked under his arm, the giant marched to the rear of the four-door car and set the kids on the bumper. Richard slumped forward and flopped to the ground. Oblivious to Richard's fall, Gary opened the trunk and removed an armload of shovels and pickaxes. Tossing them to the gravel, the rugged man grabbed Jacqueline and dumped her in the trunk. Her brother's limp body soon followed. Without a word, Gary motioned for Jacqueline to lie flat, and then he closed the trunk lid until it latched.

Darkness enveloped her world. Shuddering, Jacqueline curled into a ball and sobbed softly. A green blob floated through the air growing ever brighter. Soon, the entire interior of the trunk was illuminated.

"Xerxes Xenon and Tabitha Tantalum, I'm glad you're here," whispered Jacqueline, sniffling.

"We never departed," replied Xerxes Xenon. "As misfortune would have it, Richard was rendered unconscious, and then there were no other options but to stay. We cannot abandon Richard, and he is too heavy a burden for us element guardians to carry. Thus, we must wait until he regains consciousness."

"Listen, you can hear every word of their conversation," said Tabitha Tantalum, stroking Jacqueline's blond tresses.

"Where did that kid find the red paint?" growled Dr. James. "I'll never get it out of these clothes."

"Just like the blood you've spilled, you murderer!" shouted Dr. Ray.

"Ray, Bud, just drop it," said Gary, the sound of shovels scraping against gravel drifted through the night air. "Here, grab a pickaxe. We need to get this done. Even though we're on a desolate stretch of highway, I don't want some strangers to come wandering over that ridge, especially no cops."

"Take a lesson from Gary and learn to hold your tongue. I'd hate for anyone to meet with an accident," snarled Dr. James. "I'll search for those confounded keys while you two dig."

"Burying murder victims is not what I agreed to do. You bury him," yelled Dr. Ray.

"Dr. Ray, this is ridiculous," said Dr. James. "You will do as you are told, or we will be digging two holes tonight. The second, of course, would be for you. Do I make myself clear?

Don't answer that. Maybe the digging part was troubling you. I know it takes a little athleticism, but you can make it, Mr. Ironman. I have to listen to your triathlon stories all the time and how you swim, bike, and run for miles on end. Surely you can handle digging a little hole. It will not require that much cardio work. Now march! I don't want to hear a sound. My trigger finger is itching to squeeze off another round."

Jacqueline heard sounds of digging. Soon the sound of crunching gravel and boots shuffling through the grass and wildflowers grew fainter. Distant chirping crickets pierced the thick, steamy night air. A lone dog howled.

"I'm scared," whispered Jacqueline, wiping the perspiration from her forehead.

"I know," said Tabitha Tantalum, soothingly. "Remember how awful everything appeared when you were trapped in Greece as a slave? Well, you survived that, and you will survive this...I promise!"

"How did Richard make paint?"

"The lad must have discovered some of the other uses for chromium," replied Xerxes Xenon, removing his crown and polishing the jewels with his fingertips. "Being an astute connoisseur of the arts, I have studied numerous paintings dating to the eighteenth century. A significant number of those paintings were created with red oil paints composed predominantly of chromium elements."

"Thank you, Xerxes Xenon, for that fascinating account," said Tabitha Tantalum, laughing and shaking her head.

"I proclaim no one appreciates my noble qualities. One day you will see the folly of your ways," snorted Xerxes Xenon, puffing out his chest.

Richard groaned and attempted to roll over, but the compact trunk space restricted his movements. Tabitha Tantalum and Xerxes Xenon observed the boy with concern. Continuing to light their surroundings with his iridescence, Xerxes Xenon cast a reassuring smile at Jacqueline.

"Will Richard be okay?" asked Jacqueline, placing a hand on her brother's leg.

"Yes, but he will have one splitting headache and a nasty lump on the back of his head," replied Tabitha Tantalum. "If Dr. Kalium, with his potassium power, or if Caspar Calcium was here, one of them could ease his pain."

"I hear someone approaching," announced Xerxes Xenon, dimming the green light radiating from his body. "Listen, I detect voices."

"You know burying the body makes us an accomplice to murder," said Dr. Ray, his voice barely audible in the thick humidity.

"We're already in this too far," answered Gary. "What other choice do we have?"

"I...I don't know, but this isn't right. And what about the kids in the trunk?"

"Ray, just drop it. I'm sick of listening to all of your moral, self-righteous arguments. If you want to work at a homeless shelter or for a charity organization, do it on your own time. We have a job to do here, a job that pays extremely well. You know the consequences for failing to complete this job. So let's not analyze the ethical points of our task. Think of the payoff."

"It's blood money," muttered Dr. Ray.

"It's all green and spends the same as anyone else's money. Hey, grab the other end. We need to get this body buried and get out of here if we want to make the checkpoint in time. Those buyers won't wait for us to arrive late with the goods."

121

The two men grunted under the weight of their load. Jacqueline shivered at the crashing sound of the van door slamming shut. Heavy steps plodded past the car and eventually became inaudible.

"Where am I," mumbled Richard, reaching behind is head. "Ouch, my head is pounding. What happened?"

"You may be suffering from a slight concussion," replied Xerxes Xenon, stroking his chin. "Dr. James struck you from behind with the butt of his pistol and put you in this car trunk. To be honest, I was surprised that he failed to crack your skull. You must have quite the hard head!"

"He's known to be hard headed," giggled Jacqueline, relieved to see her brother revived.

"Very funny," grumbled Richard, gently massaging the bump on his head. "How will we ever get out of this trunk?"

"Leave that to me," answered Tabitha Tantalum. "By the power of the transition metals, I summon tantalum!" sang the petite element, emitting a glowing orb from her palms.

An orb floated between Tabitha Tantalum's hands. Closing her eyes, she tilted her head back and hummed softly. Glowing more brightly, the sphere pulsed with energy. Within seconds, the orb metamorphosed into a blinding flame and then vanished. Opening her eyes and looking at her hands, Tabitha Tantalum held two thin strips of gray metal.

"Wow, that was so cool!" gasped Jacqueline, rubbing her eyes.

"Oh, that was nothing," assured Tabitha Tantalum, drifting to the trunk's lock. "Compared to creating surgical equipment, aircraft and missile components, and pieces for camera lenses, making these tantalum strips was quite simple. I should be able to pick this lock and get us out of here."

122

Tabitha Tantalum removed a thin plate of metal from the rear panel and dropped it on the trunk floor. Hunched over the tiny lock, she pried at the apparatus with the two pieces of metal. Jacqueline watched the element intently and shuddered excitedly when a click reverberated through the interior of their crude prison.

"Richard, push against the trunk lid," directed Tabitha Tantalum, backing away from the lock.

Cautiously, Richard applied pressure against the lid. Nothing moved. Placing both hands firmly against the cold metal, Richard pressed harder. The trunk lid flew upward and bounced back toward the siblings. Swiftly kicking his leg up, Richard caught the lid, preventing it from closing.

"Could we make any more noise?" asked Xerxes Xenon, rolling his eyes.

"The coast is clear," announced Tabitha Tantalum, standing on the trunk's lip.

Groggily rising to a seated position, Richard peered into the darkness. His eyes slowly adjusted and focused on the distant, black outline of a figure beating through the underbrush with a stick. Pointing wildly at the thin figure, Richard looked questioningly at the elements.

Nodding her head, Tabitha Tantalum motioned for the children to exit the trunk. "That's Dr. James. He's looking for the van keys, which Jacqueline threw into the ravine. He won't even notice us."

Smiling and gesturing with a thumbs-up to his sister, Richard clambered out of the trunk. Planting both feet in the gravel, Richard attempted to stand, but he could not shake the dizzy spell overwhelming him. Swaying to his left, he overcorrected and lost his balance, plummeting face first to the gravel. Spitting pebbles, he gave a half smile and pulled himself into a crouched position behind the car. Jacqueline quickly followed and bent over next to her brother, rubbing his shoulders. Xerxes Xenon hovered before the children. Rising to his feet but remaining slightly bent at the waist, Richard grabbed the trunk lid and lowered it like a fragile plate of glass until it quietly clicked closed. Exhaling, he tapped his sister on the shoulder and motioned for her to follow.

The small group tiptoed across the barren shoulder and crouched in a thick clump of shrubbery. Peeking from their concealed location, Richard searched for the tall shadowy figure. Unable to locate the doctor, Richard grew frantic.

"Where is..." began Jacqueline, in a muffled whisper noticing her brother's wide-eyed expression.

A twig snapped and pebbles scattered across the ground. Dr. James' saddle-oxford wing-tip shoes protruded from the darkness within inches of the childrens' hiding spot. Rising up on his toes and arching his back, Dr. James stretched and sighed loudly. Walking with a long gait, he swiftly covered the distance between the siblings' hideout and the car.

Beating on the trunk lid with his clenched fist, Dr. James snarled, "Very cute, throwing the keys in the ravine. Too bad it won't save your life. You urchins will pay dearly for your disrespect, and to make it even more fun, I'll let you wait until we reach our destination. Do you hear me in there?" he shouted at the trunk lid. "I guess you're too scared to answer. Silence is a much more suitable virtue for someone of your inexperience and youth. Unfortunately for you, you're never too young to die."

Chuckling, Dr. James circled the car and opened the passenger side door. Stepping away from the car, he sauntered to the van and yanked open the rear door. The wiry doctor reached far into the van and retrieved the cooler. Slamming the door, he made his way to the car and placed the cooler on the passenger-side floorboard.

"Hey, Doc, are you ready?" asked Gary, climbing up the incline to the gravel-covered shoulder of the road.

"That was quick. How did you bury the body so fast?"

"Oh, we found an uprooted pine tree that had left an extremely deep hole. All we had to do was dump the body and shovel in some rocks and dirt. It's the easiest burial I've ever performed. Did you find the keys?"

"No, those rotten kids will pay for it though. We'll take the car; after we make the trade, I'll get the spare set of keys from the office. We've got plenty of time to make it to the old municipal airport."

"What do I do with these tools?" asked Gary, holding out a shovel and pickaxe. "I don't want to open the trunk and get sprayed with paint like you."

"Oh, you're hilarious! Quite the comedian. Keep it up, and it'll cost you your share of our take on the organs. Never mind the trunk, just let Dr. Ray hold the tools in the back seat. It'll make him feel productive without having to compromise his high moral standards."

Guffawing loudly, the two men flashed wicked smiles at Dr. Ray. Without a word, the doctor grabbed the tools from Gary and flung them into the back seat. All three men clambered into the car. Within seconds, the vehicle roared to life. Its tail lights flickered like narrow red eyes glaring at the concealed children. The tires spun, firing gravel and pebble bullets at the childrens' hiding place. The car lurched forward to the smooth highway blacktop and the tail lights' red eyes quickly faded, leaving the children in stark darkness.

"They're gone!" blurted Jacqueline, breathing more freely.

Inhaling sharply, Jacqueline stared at her brother through large saucer-like eyes. She swallowed hard and breathed in short rapid bursts. Through moist eyes, the young girl nervously scanned the eerie blackness surrounding her.

"Jacqueline, are you okay?" asked Richard.

"Where are we? We're lost. How are we getting back?" cried Jacqueline, with tears streaming down her face in tiny rivers. "We're stuck in the middle of nowhere with creepy noises and shadows. What if Dr. James comes looking for us? We're dead. What are we going to do? Help!"

"Don't panic," said Tabitha Tantalum, climbing onto Jacqueline's shoulder and wiping her tears with the hem of her cloak. "I know today's events have been upsetting, and that has made you extremely emotional. However, we must remain calm and keep our wits about us."

"Tabitha Tantalum is correct. We must keep our wits about us. In fact, we made it through much greater perils when we were trapped in ancient Greece," proclaimed Xerxes Xenon, his arm slowly sweeping the air in grand arcs.

"Yeah, take a sedative. You're about to hyperventilate on us. Get a grip!" said Richard, reassuringly grabbing his sister's arm. "We'll find some way out of here even if we have to find those van keys and drive out of here."

"The keys," shouted Jacqueline, springing from her hiding place in the shrubbery. "I know where the keys landed. When I threw them, they slipped out of the side of my hand and flew under a blackberry bush."

"Are you serious? We're saved. Let's find those keys," exclaimed Richard, racing past his sister.

"Dr. James must have thought I threw them a long way because he was looking too far down the bank for them," continued Jacqueline, trailing her brother to the guardrail. "There's the blackberry bush. They went in there."

"Hey, Xerxes Xenon, could you give us some light over here?" asked Richard, climbing over the railing and sliding down the embankment until he reached the thorny bush.

"How dare you address me as a lower-class servant? Simply hollering my name as if I were a playmate of yours or a domesticated canine," scolded Xerxes Xenon, drifting toward Richard. "I am not a flashlight. I expect in the future that you will regard me with greater respect, the respect befitting one of such a noble stature as myself. And furthermore..."

"I'm sorry," interjected Richard, slowly shaking his head. "I got a little excited and didn't think about what I was saying."

"That is quite understandable considering our current situation," said Xerxes Xenon, a green beam shining from each of his fists illuminating the plant. "I shall pardon you of all your injustices. Look, there at the end of my beam. Those are the keys flashing in the light. We found them!" yelled Xerxes Xenon, neglecting to maintain his noble demeanor in the moment of excitement.

"I've got them. Ouch!" groaned Richard, snagging his arm on one of the numerous thorns extending from the blackberry bush. "These thorns hurt. Does anyone have a knife? Never mind, I've got it. We're getting out of here, now," whooped Richard, removing his arm from the briar patch and jingling the keys before him.

"Great work," yelled Tabitha Tantalum from the guardrail. "With a little team effort, we can survive anything.

Okay, while Xerxes Xenon returns to the hospital to get help and to tell the others, we'll drive to the airport."

"The airport?" asked Jacqueline, her hands trembling.

"The hospital?" asked Xerxes Xenon, extinguishing the rays emitting from his fists and placing his hands on his hips. "If you think I am flying all the way back to the hospital, you had better reconsider your options. Elements may be able to move quickly, but a trip to the hospital is a long journey even for an element unless you happen to be that spastic Ned Nitrogen. Unfortunately, he is sleeping in the recovery room."

"Xerxes Xenon, I don't wish to be rude, but you could stand to lose a few pounds as it is. So consider the trip to the hospital a positive step for your health. Besides, we can't allow Dr. James to get away with murder. Someone has to keep track of him. If we all drive to the hospital, it would be too late for us to do anything. And I'm sure Dr. James would try to find Richard and Jacqueline because they know what he has done. We have to stop the doctor, but we're going to need more help. The only people who will listen to us are back at the hospital. I don't see where we have any other options."

"Okay, you have made your point," grumbled Xerxes Xenon, flustered. "I am leaving. I can perceive when I am not wanted," he snorted. "By the way, in all of your grand scheming, do not forget to memorize or make a note of that mile marker up the road. Otherwise, we will not be able to tell the authorities where to look for the evidence, the body those criminals buried."

"Thank you, Xerxes Xenon. We will do that. Have a safe trip," said Tabitha Tantalum, waving.

Without another word, Xerxes Xenon vanished into the darkness. His head drooping and his chest fallen, Richard

stood quietly with the keys dangling at his side. Tabitha Tantalum anxiously observed the two devastated children.

"Everything will work out. I promise," reassured Tabitha Tantalum.

"I thought we'd finally be able to go home," said Richard, raising his head.

"You will be going home as soon as we collar Dr. James. Actually, we'll save the arresting part for the police. But we have to keep track of his whereabouts, so the police can arrest him."

"Can't we just call them and tell them?" asked Jacqueline.

"It would be too late," said Tabitha Tantalum. "Besides, when Dr. James opens the trunk and discovers that you two have escaped, he will be coming to look for you. He won't stop hunting until he has found you, even if he has to go to your house. Evildoers like Dr. James don't leave witnesses alive. And you two are witnesses."

"I don't know what to do. I'm so scared!"

"Me, too, Jacqueline. But Tabitha Tantalum is right. We can't stop here," said Richard, hurdling the railing. "We're only going to spy on Dr. James. We'll stay hidden. He'll never know we're there."

"If you say so," sighed Jacqueline, skeptically. "Um, when was the last time you drove?"

"Uh, about a month ago," squeaked Richard, unfurling a crooked half smile.

"I'm not feeling much confidence in your driving skills, Brother. Or, should I say, your lack of driving abilities. Maybe Tabitha Tantalum should take the wheel," suggested Jacqueline, hesitantly following her brother to the van.

"The steering wheel is about all I could take," answered Tabitha Tantalum, giggling. "I could never reach the pedals. It's up to Richard. All I can suggest is to drive slowly."

"I will," promised Richard, opening the driver's door and hopping onto the seat.

Slowly, Jacqueline climbed into the passenger seat, mumbling, "What do I have to lose? I can't stay here. I either die in a car wreck or wait here for Dr. James to come back. I think I'll choose the wreck."

"Thanks, Jacqueline. Your confidence is overwhelming," replied Richard, inserting the key into the ignition.

With a flick of the fifteen-year old's wrist, the sleeping van awakened. Like a sickly person, it sputtered and coughed before roaring to life. Tapping the accelerator with his foot, Richard gripped the shift stick.

"Here goes nothing," said Richard, shifting the vehicle out of park.

Releasing the brake, Richard pressed the accelerator. The van rocked backward throwing Jacqueline against the dashboard. Stomping on the brake, the blushing youth looked sheepishly at his sister.

"Sorry. Are you hurt?"

"No, I'm fine. Next time, try putting it in forward instead of reverse. The airport is the other way. I'll be lucky to be in one piece by the time you get this van on the road," answered Jacqueline, sliding back in her seat and reaching for the seat belt strap.

"See, you should have been wearing your seat belt. Don't look at me like that. I'm only kidding. I'll try again," said Richard, shifting the van into drive.

"Turn on your lights," said Jacqueline, clutching the elbow rest and giggling.

"What's so funny? Would you rather drive?"

"No, this is going to be the best ride of my life," answered Jacqueline, laughing.

Grinning, Richard stepped on the pedal. The truck's wheels spun, flinging dirt and gravel. Finally, the wheels caught and the truck jumped onto the highway. Swerving in and out of the lane, the van veered from side to side.

"Keep it between the lines!" said Jacqueline, between bouts of laughter.

"I'm trying. It's hard to steer though. Would you quit laughing and read that mile marker over there."

"Okay, I...I got it."

"I did, too. Remember mile marker 31," added Tabitha Tantalum, amused by Richard's driving. "This trip in the van will be a great story to tell the other elements later."

"Very funny," replied Richard, tightly clutching the steering wheel. "By the way, which way is it to the airport?"

"Straight ahead," answered Tabitha Tantalum, sitting on the front seat and reclining against Jacqueline's thigh.

"Thank goodness. That means I don't have to make any turns."

Laughing uproariously, the two children bounced up and down on the seats, feeling every bump on the narrow stretch of asphalt. The stripes on the road zipped past the truck, blurring into a single line. Squinting, Richard stared into the darkness attempting to see beyond the headlights and farther into the wispy, rolling fog settling upon the highway.

In time the van found a straighter course and ceased its perilous swerving. The laughter slowly faded, permitting fatigue to grab hold of the two weary youngsters. Through drooping eyelids, Richard watched the road, seeing little and hearing only the whistling wind penetrating the many crevices and cracks in the van.

Relaxing her grip on the arm rest, Jacqueline glanced at Tabitha Tantalum. The tiny element yawned and stretched. Returning her attention to the road, Jacqueline ran her fingers through her hair and arched her back until it popped and cracked. She inhaled deeply and gradually exhaled one lengthy breath. Leaning forward in her seat, Jacqueline pointed at a sign to the right of the truck.

"What is it?" asked Tabitha Tantalum, startling Richard who jerked the wheel causing the vehicle to career sharply to the right.

"Whoa, take it easy!" urged Jacqueline, pressing her forehead against the window and squinting at the sign. "It says fifteen miles to the airport."

"And fifteen miles to Dr. James," said Richard, shuddering as an eerie silence fell over the van.

# "Ozone"

"Ozzie Ozone, wait!" pleaded Ollie Oxygen. "You can't win by attacking Clifton Chlorine. Remember the laws of chemistry and thermodynamics. You do not have enough strength down here in the lower atmosphere to wage a war against Clifton Chlorine."

"Ollie Oxygen makes a valid point," agreed Dr. Kalium. "There is not enough solar radiation to cause photo ionization, or the separation of oxygen molecules near the earth's surface. Photons, which are tiny particles of light, can have extremely short wavelengths. The short wavelengths of light are almost completely filtered out of the radiation from the sun in the upper atmosphere where ozone chiefly resides. Thus, photons that are left in the light reaching us don't have enough energy to separate the $O_2$ molecules into oxygen atoms. That's a good thing because if the photons reaching us still had that much energy, humans, plants, and animals would not survive very well. "

"I understand the process. I know what happens in the upper atmosphere. As you said, I live there. What is your point?" asked Ozzie Ozone, green vapor leaking from between his blackened, worn teeth.

"Your anger has clouded your mind," said Ollie Oxygen, raising his voice.

"You can't even think. What good are you doing the ozone molecules that you are supposed to protect?"

"Do not cross me, Ollie Oxygen," thundered Ozzie Ozone. "I have no quarrel with you, but don't step over the line. You know your place."

"Yes, I know my place," said Ollie Oxygen. "But do you remember yours? Have you forgotten the role I play in your very existence? I create you. You're made of nothing more than oxygen atoms. As you should recall, oxygen normally exists as a diatomic molecule, that is, a molecule consisting of two of the same elements. The diatomic molecule of oxygen known as "$O_2$" is what humans and all animals breathe. But ozone also needs $O_2$ because every time $O_2$ collides with a free oxygen atom, the "O" element, an ozone, or $O_3$ molecule is created."

"Your problem, Ozzie Ozone, is that no "O" or oxygen atoms are floating around here," said Dr. Kalium, distracting Ozzie Ozone's attention and rage from Ollie Oxygen. "Look around. The only oxygen element not attached to another oxygen element is Ollie Oxygen because he is a guardian. All of the solar radiation that has enough energy to separate the oxygen molecules into single oxygen atoms has been absorbed high in the sky, in the stratosphere. Only a lightning strike could generate enough energy to split the oxygen molecules this close to the earth's surface."

"I don't need any more oxygen. I already have enough ozone to destroy that puny element," growled Ozzie Ozone, pointing a gnarled, bony finger at Clifton Chlorine.

"Are you sure you have enough ozone?" asked Ollie Oxygen, stepping closer to Ozzie Ozone. "Did you also forget how easily ozone separates or as chemists say, "photodisassociates," into an oxygen molecule and an oxygen atom? Any photon, or light particle, with a wavelength shorter than eleven-hundred-forty nanometers has enough energy to destroy you. Look at the lights in the ceiling above your head. They are radiating light in the visible light spectrum, which has wavelengths longer than eleven-hundred-forty nanometers.

"Ozzie Ozone, you are falling apart," said Dr. Kalium. "You are much thinner than you were earlier today. In fact, you are nothing more than a skeleton beneath those tattered robes. In addition, the only life forms you are harming are the children. Your gas is toxic to them, not to mention the annoyingly sharp, peppery smell. Take a look at the kids' teary eyes and flushed faces," he said, pointing to Catherine, Jeanne-Marie, and Anthony huddled inside the doorway with their hands clamped over their noses.

"Remember, chlorine reacts rapidly with ozone to form oxygen, $O_2$, and chlorine monoxide, $ClO$, which destroys ozone," said Ollie Oxygen. "But the only way chlorine can travel into the upper atmosphere is to combine with carbon and fluorine elements to form the chlorofluorocarbons, CFCs, found in spray cans and refrigerant and air-conditioner gases, and used as foaming agents for plastics. Once these chlorofluorocarbons, or CFCs, reach the stratosphere, the short wavelengths of the high-energy solar radiation cause photodisassociation. In other words, the high-energy photons in sunlight break the bonds between the fluorine, carbon, and chlorine elements. This frees the chlorine elements, allowing them to destroy the ozone and form chlorine monoxide. Get the picture?" asked Ollie Oxygen, floating upward until he stared directly into the eyes of Ozzie Ozone.

"You have made your point, but I will not leave until I have made sure no chlorine atoms survive to float into my stratosphere," snarled Ozzie Ozone.

"Wake up! That has already been done," said Ollie Oxygen. "The 1990 Clean Air Act mandated that CFC production cease in the year 2000. However, in February 1992 increasing evidence of ozone depletion or reduction in your stratosphere prompted President George Bush to move this deadline forward to 1995. Everyone, including humans, is trying to help you," he said. "Forget about Clifton Chlorine. He is nothing more than a pest who will be spending much time in Molecule Prison. We will handle him. You should spend your time repairing and rebuilding the ozone layer."

"For now I will heed what you suggest. But don't let me catch another chlorine atom in my stratosphere! I don't want to hear another word from anybody. I'm tired, and I'm going home," seethed Ozzie Ozone, vanishing in a blinding flash of lightening and a cloud of pungent green gas.

"The mighty Ozzie Ozone has fled!" snickered Clifton Chlorine, sneering.

"Another word from you, and we'll discover just how mighty you are," scolded Dr. Kalium. "I will transfer this villain to Molecule Prison. See you soon," said the doctor, waving and vanishing with Clifton Chlorine.

"I can't believe we survived," gasped Catherine, crouching.

"Yeah, we should get T-shirts printed with 'I survived Clifton Chlorine and Ozzie Ozone,'" replied Anthony, tilting his head and staring at the ceiling. "I don't want to see either of them again. I don't think my heart could have taken much more. This was scarier than any Halloween!"

"Yes, but did you notice how much less painful it was to reason with Ozzie Ozone than to physically fight with him or Clifton Chlorine? No one was seriously injured. Even Caspar Calcium is okay," said Catherine.

The tiny atom raised a trembling hand and waved at the children. Rising to a seated position, the dazed element pressed his chin against his chest. Caspar Calcium sat in the middle of the floor and groggily observed his surroundings. Drawing his feet beneath him, he stood up on his two wobbly legs. The "Ca" tattooed on his chest rose and fell with each breath. Ollie Oxygen handed Caspar Calcium his spear, which served as an instant crutch.

"He needs some time to shake the cobwebs from his head, but he'll come around," said Ollie Oxygen. "I hope the three of you learned something from this tragic experience. The next time any of you becomes angry, take a moment to think through the problem. There is always a peaceful solution that can save you from pain and even death," he said, motioning for the threesome to follow him down the hallway. "I think it is time for a little rest for all of us."

"Rest? There is no time for leisure or repose," said Xerxes Xenon, appearing before the group.

"Xerxes Xenon, what are you doing here?" asked Jeanne-Marie, holding her sister's hand.

Panting, Xerxes Xenon continued, "Richard, Jacqueline, and Tabitha Tantalum are following Dr. James to the municipal airport. Everything is out of control! Dr. James not only committed murder, but he has been stealing and selling human organs illegally. Dr. Ray and another criminal are helping him. And they even captured Richard and Jacqueline but the children managed to escape. Once Dr. James discovers them missing, he will stop at nothing to hunt them down and to kill them."

"Slow down, Xerxes Xenon. You're about to faint," said Ollie Oxygen, fanning Xerxes Xenon with his cape.

"We must call nine-one-one and inform the authorities. Somehow, we have to sneak out of the hospital and transport ourselves to the airport," said Xerxes Xenon.

"I agree," replied Ollie Oxygen. "Let's take this one step at a time. No one panic."

"I'll call nine-one-one if you tell me what to say," volunteered Anthony, stepping forward.

"Great, I believe there is a phone next door," said Xerxes Xenon, doubling over at the waist and breathing heavily through his mouth. "We will meet you behind the hospital. Try to find some mode of transportation. Make haste!"

Without waiting for a reply, Xerxes Xenon led Anthony into the vacant room. Silently Catherine and Jeanne-Marie trailed Ollie Oxygen down the hall. Caspar Calcium nodded approvingly and waved good-bye. Draping her arm across Jeanne-Marie's shoulders, Catherine gave her a comforting squeeze.

"There's the exit straight ahead," said Ollie Oxygen.

"Are you sure we should leave the hospital?" asked Catherine, shuddering. "The thought of running into Dr. James makes my skin crawl! There must be another way to do this."

"If there is another way, I'd be more than happy to hear it. Did you have another idea?"

"No," murmured Catherine, crossing her arms across her chest and staring aimlessly at the floor. "I was hoping you had another idea. Oh, well, we can't leave Richard and Jacqueline stranded at the airport. Somebody has to save them."

"You sound very encouraging. Don't be too eager," teased Ollie Oxygen, smiling. "Whatever happened to your adventuresome spirit?"

139

"I think with all the excitement today, my spirit has flown away."

"Where'd it go?" asked Jeanne-Marie, peering up at Catherine through large, round eyes.

"Oh, nowhere. We're only kidding," said Catherine, forcing a smile and hugging Jeanne-Marie.

"Hey, wait," yelled Anthony, racing down the hall with Xerxes Xenon.

"Don't yell," warned Ollie Oxygen.

Panting, Anthony skidded to a halt before his sisters, "nine-one-one told us to wait at the hospital."

"Why at the hospital?"

"Because they traced our call to the hospital. They said a police officer would be here shortly and would take us to the airport. I'm not sure if she believed our whole story. It is an amazing tale with the organ smuggling and all."

"There's no time to wait. Where did the police tell you to meet them?"

"In the main lobby," answered Anthony.

"Okay, then, we're going to the main lobby," said Ollie Oxygen, leading the group along a side corridor to a row of shiny elevators.

"What about the airport?" asked Catherine, hoping they would wait for the police.

"That's where we're headed. But first we need to leave a message for the police with the receptionist. I have a premonition, or feeling, that the police may not take this too seriously. But they will check it out. It may be too late by the time they get to the airport if we don't do something."

The elevator chimed and the "Up" arrow lit. The doors slowly parted revealing an empty elevator. Stepping inside and gripping the metal handrail, Catherine rose onto her toes and pressed the button labeled "2." The elevator jerked and moved upward at a snail's pace, stopping at the first floor. Catherine impatiently tapped her foot but stopped abruptly when the doors slid open. An elderly white-haired woman clothed in blue pants and a pink coat stared at the sun glass-clad children and cautiously entered the elevator.

"You poor dears, are you from the second ward?" asked the woman, in a gentle tone.

"Pardon me, Ma'am, what did you say?" asked Anthony, nervously rubbing his hands against his pants' legs and looking at Catherine.

"I'm over here, Honey. I know it's difficult being blind, but you are so brave. My late husband was in an accident several years before he passed away. The wreck left him temporarily blind, and we had the most awful time doing simple, everyday tasks. I admire your courage."

"We're not..."

"Oh, then you must be part of the Blind Awareness Group, visiting the children in the blind ward. Your presence is invaluable. Those kids think of you as role models. By letting them know that you live normal lives, it gives them hope and inspiration."

"How..."

"Oh, by your sunglasses, Sweetie. That's how I knew you were sight impaired. I believe the rest of your group is already on the bus. It's about to leave for the Municipal Airport. I don't want you to miss the bus or your flight to Denver. I believe that's where your driver mentioned you were headed. It's good you're flying because it's a long drive to Denver. Here, take my hand, and I'll lead you to the bus," said the woman, grabbing Catherine's hand.

"But, Ma'am..."

"Oh, Honey, you don't have to call me ma'am. Although, it is nice to hear someone using manners in this day and age. Kids these days don't respect their elders like they did in the past. There was a time when respect and family meant so much more. Now everyone is too busy or self-centered to find time to enjoy their families and to spend time learning from elders. Oh, my, listen to me ramble on and on. I do apologize. My name is Mrs. Brook..."

"I didn't plan for this, but it will get us to the airport," whispered Ollie Oxygen. "When we get on the bus, don't talk to anyone because they will immediately know we're not part of the group," he said, watching the elevator doors part.

"Anthony, walk slowly. We need to wait until the woman is far enough ahead of us that she cannot hear us. Then you can leave a message with the receptionist," said Xerxes Xenon, hovering above Anthony.

The woman, bent with age, guided Catherine, who clutched Jeanne-Marie's hand, through the lobby. Smiling at nurses and hospital employees, the elderly lady failed to notice Anthony ambling toward the front desk. Catherine glanced over her shoulder and nodded to her brother motioning for him to hurry. The elderly woman continued her lively chatter oblivious to Catherine and Anthony motioning to one another.

*How do we get ourselves into these situations?* thought Catherine, feeling the old woman's warm hand beneath hers. *There has to be something wrong with impersonating a blind person. This isn't right, but there is no other way for us to find transportation to the airport. None of us can drive, and Richard and Jacqueline are in horrible danger. What if Dr. James shoots them? That's an awful thought. I've never seen anyone walk as slowly as this lady. She must think blind people can't walk because they can't see. Oh, well, she's just trying to be helpful. I'm sure she's very nice. She's probably somebody's grandmother. I just have to remain calm. Oh, I can hear Anthony's voice. I hope he hurries!*

"Yes, Ma'am," answered Anthony, drumming nervously on the counter with his fingertips. "The police want to meet with Anthony. They will be here soon. Just tell them he has already left for the airport. They'll know what you're talking about. Anthony will meet them there."

"And what's your name, young man?" asked the receptionist, scribbling the message on a yellow legal pad.

"Uh, um...Richard," replied Anthony, glancing at Xerxes Xenon who chuckled.

"Okay, I've got it all here."

"Thank you," said Anthony, turning and jogging through the lobby until he reached the front door where the woman was exiting with his sisters.

"Step down, Dear" said the lady. "This is a high curb. Great, I'm glad we're all still together. Now, we have only about thirty more paces to the bus. It's a lovely bus, too."

*She's so optimistic*, thought Catherine, staring at the faded blue bus. *I'll bet everything is beautiful to her. I hope we don't get caught. I wonder if you could go to jail for pretending to be blind. We'll just tell them this was a school assignment to teach us respect for the blind. When will this day ever end?*

"Here we are, safe and sound. I'll guide your hand to the railing. Then all you have is three steps until you've reached the inside of the bus. Turn left at the top of the steps. Have a safe trip and take care of yourselves," said the woman, hugging each of the children. "My, those are unusual but beautiful sunglasses you kids are wearing. Bye, bye, dears."

The thin, frail woman turned and hobbled toward the hospital, massaging her lower back. Catherine observed the rows of seats filled with men and women wearing sunglasses and holding white canes. Most were engaged in quiet conversations and paid no attention to the arrival of the newcomers. Anthony gently pushed Catherine forward and the threesome made their way to the back of the bus. Finding an empty seat at the rear of the vehicle, Catherine and her brother and sister slumped down far enough in the seat so as not to be seen from the front of the bus. Ollie Oxygen and Xerxes Xenon sat on the top of the back seat surveying the travelers. Jeanne-Marie tightly clamped onto Catherine's arm.

After an agonizing couple of minutes, the driver sprang onto the bus, "Are we ready?"

"Yes!" yelled several passengers.

"Let's move 'em out. There's a plane waiting for us!"

The doors clamped shut, and the driver shifted the bus into low gear. Releasing the air brakes with a loud "Whoosh," the vehicle lurched forward. Rolling out of the parking lot, the roar of the bus made speaking and hearing difficult. Straightening in her seat, Catherine peered out the window at the passing landscape and wondered if her brother and sister shared her fears of being captured by Dr. James.

# "Municipal Airport"

"Turn!" screamed Jacqueline. Her face was pressed against the window, watching in vain as the van streaked past the exit.

"Don't worry about it. Take the next exit," instructed Tabitha Tantalum, standing on the dashboard. "It's after this overpass. Slow down. You don't want to turn too quickly, or you could tip us over."

"Could you drop me off here, and I'll meet you at the airport?" asked Jacqueline, giggling.

"Very funny, this isn't a taxi service. Be glad you're not driving," replied Richard, concentrating on the upcoming exit.

"Trust me, I would much rather be the passenger than the driver."

"Ease off the accelerator and coast onto the exit ramp," said Tabitha Tantalum. "I wish this fog would lift. It would make seeing much easier."

"Which way do I go?" asked Richard, pressing the brake with his foot.

"Left. Loop under the highway and turn left at the intersection. That'll put us on Airline Road."

"I can handle this."

Jacqueline reclined in her seat pondering her fears. *This is it. We're here. I guess there's no turning back. I ought to tell Tabitha Tantalum that we should go to the main lobby and call the police. But she'll have some reason why we shouldn't. How there isn't enough time, how Dr. James and*

*Dr. Ray will get away before the police can get here, how we have to catch them in the act. I'm not into all this hero stuff. But I have to be brave or my brothers will never let me hear the end of it. Maybe Anthony, Catherine, or even Jeanne-Marie called the cops.*

"What are you thinking?" asked Tabitha Tantalum, observing Jacqueline from her seated position on the dashboard with her legs dangling over the edge.

"Oh, nothing," replied Jacqueline, shifting in her seat.

"Good. You were too quiet for a moment there. I wanted to make sure you are okay."

Jacqueline nodded and silently watched the rolling scenery. As the van turned under the highway the landscape shifted from wooded thickets to open fields dotted with various aircraft. A low-flying Cessna soared above the van on its final approach to the runway.

"That's probably the type of plane Dr. James is meeting," said Tabitha Tantalum. "It has to be a small private plane. There is no way he could be smuggling the organs onto a large commercial flight. I doubt he would risk such a dangerous maneuver."

"Which way do we go?" asked Richard, coasting slowly along the road leading into the airport.

"See that sign at the split in the road?"

"Yep."

"The arrow pointing left leads to the private airfield, and the one to the right is commercial. Take the left road."

"Wow, look at all of the planes. How are we ever going to find Dr. James?" asked Jacqueline, staring at the rows of Pipers, Cessnas, and private jets separated from the road by a ten-foot-high wire fence.

"Keep your eyes peeled. They're around here some-where."

"Over there," said Richard, his voice hushed, tense.

"It's the car!" gasped Jacqueline, slumping in her seat.

"Turn off your lights," instructed Tabitha Tantalum. "Park on the side of that hangar ahead of us. We want to be out of sight in case they come back to the car. If Dr. James spots his van, he'll know we're here."

Easing the vehicle into the low-cropped grass alongside the hangar, Richard cut the engine. Tabitha Tantalum hopped from the dashboard and climbed onto Jacqueline's shoulder. Nodding to his sister, Richard cautiously opened his door and stepped from the van. Pressing the door closed, careful to avoid making any sounds, Richard walked gingerly around the truck to join his sister on the passenger side.

"Close your door," hissed Richard. "Someone will see the cabin light."

"Oh!" blurted Jacqueline, slamming the door with a resounding crash.

"Jacqueline..."

"Who's there?"

A harsh masculine voice froze the children like a deer transfixed by headlights. The sound of shuffling boots reverberated from inside the hangar, drawing ever closer to Richard and Jacqueline. Frantically waving her arms, Tabitha Tantalum attempted to snap the petrified children from their trance. A metal door to the left of Jacqueline flew open, revealing a shadowy figure framed by the doorway. Stepping out of the hangar and into the light cast by the airport's numerous powerful lights the man paused.

"It's the van!" shouted Gary, shocked. "Hey, you kids, how'd you get here? What's going on? Something funny is

147

happening. No matter, Dr. James sent me back to get you two anyway. It's time for a plane ride. On the way you can explain how you got out of the trunk and what the van's doing here. It's a good thing I took a short cut through the hangar or you might have slipped past me. Now put your hands on top of your head."

Spurred by Gary's sharp tone, Richard instinctively followed orders placing his hands on top of his head. Jacqueline did not move. Gary stepped toward the two intimidated youngsters.

"Use your rings!" urged Tabitha Tantalum, spreading her arms before her. "Never mind, I'll do it. Although tantalum is used for good in the replacement of bones such as in hip joints, may it once again free us from our oppressors!"

A pinpoint of light appeared and rapidly transformed into a glowing orb the size of a basketball. Hovering before Tabitha Tantalum, the ball of light rose until it floated before the unsuspecting man. Inching closer, Gary scowled at the motionless children, then paused, confused by the two sibling's stunned, trance-like state.

Humming softly, Tabitha Tantalum closed her eyes and lowered her head. The miniature element held her upturned palms before her. Gradually, she raised her head and opened her eyes. Staring skyward, she clapped her hands together. The orb radiated brightly, then erupted in a ball of flames plunging thin, metal needles into Gary's face. The burly man screamed and recoiled, falling to the short-clipped, Bermuda grass. Clawing at his throbbing face, Gary struggled to remove the splinters.

Snapping to her senses, Jacqueline slapped Richard on his stomach, "Use your chromium power!"

"Ye...yes, you're right," replied Richard, removing his hands from the top of his head.

Gary fell on his back and kicked his feet in the dirt. Howling, he pulled at his hair and scratched his face. Richard pointed his clenched fist at the writhing man. The red ruby in his ring gleamed in the light.

"By the mysteries of the transition elements, I summon chromium!" yelled Richard.

"What..." began Gary, startled by Richard's outburst.

His words were cut short by the flash of silver erupting from Richard's ring. The silver streak wrapped itself around Gary's wrist and ankles. Within seconds, the silver converted into a reflective strip of metal binding Gary's wrists to his ankles.

"How'd you do that?' asked Gary, his voice quivering.

"It's our secret; but if you holler, you'll see plenty more!" yelled Jacqueline, her heart pounding rapidly.

"Tell him if he sits quietly, the stinging in his face will stop," said Tabitha Tantalum, bowing her head and humming softly.

"Gary, I believe that is your name, or at least that's what the other guys called you, if you will be quiet and sit still, the stinging in your face will stop," said Jacqueline, crossing her arms.

"Whatever you say," replied Gary, rolling over and lying in the shadows cast by the hangar. "I...I've heard of aliens before...but I never believed it until now. Please don't hurt me. I'm only a harmless Earthling. Ouch, ouch, my face won't stop burning!"

Tabitha Tantalum raised her head and gazed into the eyes of the shivering man. Raising her arms, she ceased her humming and clapped her hands together. Gary's face glowed brilliantly and then flickered like a flame being blown by the wind.

"Hey, the pain stopped. Oh, thank you! I promise to be quiet. I'll wait here. You won't hear a peep from me," whimpered Gary, continuing to shiver in the hot night.

*I can't believe how scared he is*, thought Jacqueline, watching the large man in amusement. *With the help of the elements and our rings, we can do anything. Let's find Dr. James.*

"Ask him where the others are," instructed Tabitha Tantalum.

"Where are Dr. James and Dr. Ray?" asked Richard, standing over Gary.

"At the end of the second tarmac; they're loading the plane."

"We'll see you later," said Richard, grabbing his sister's hand and dragging her into the hangar. "What's a tarmac?"

"It's the runway," answered Tabitha Tantalum. "You two did a great job back there. You were very brave, but don't let your powers make you conceited. If you become overconfident, you will make mistakes. Dr. James has a gun with bullets, and he is not afraid to use it. Let's remember caution. Speaking of remembering, Richard, you do recall you can use your ring only three times in a twenty-four-hour period?"

"Aw, I forgot about that. My ring is useless until tomorrow. It's up to you, Jacqueline."

"Great," whispered Jacqueline, no longer feeling sure of her abilities. "I can't believe he called us aliens. Like we're from some science fiction movie or from another planet. No wonder we can't let anyone know about the secrets of the elements. They would think we are freaks and lock us up somewhere. The government might even study us thinking we are from outer space."

"Jacqueline, let's try to think positive thoughts. We've got enough to worry about for now," said Richard, exiting the hangar and surveying the rows of runways stretching through the grassy acreage.

"Those planes are huge," said Jacqueline, pointing across the field.

"Yeah, I think we need to go the other way to the smaller planes."

"I see three guys at the end of the second short runway walking around that plane."

"That's it. You've got good eyes, Jacqueline. Circle around behind them so we can hide between those two planes lining the tarmac," said Tabitha Tantalum, resting on Jacqueline's shoulder. "We need to stay out of sight."

"What's the plan?"

"I'm working on it. Stopping three guys is not going to be easy."

"Who's the third guy?"

"He must be the pilot. Watch your step."

Crouching close to the ground, the children approached the three dark figures. Oblivious to the siblings' presence, the men quarreled loudly, but Richard and Jacqueline were not close enough to hear what they were saying. Dropping to his belly, Richard led his sister toward the two empty planes parked along the tarmac like sentinels.

Creeping through the grass, Jacqueline trembled. *Maybe now would be a good time to call for help,*" she thought. *What can we do against three grown men, especially when Richard's ring doesn't work? This is suicide! How do we get stuck in these crazy situations?*

# "Municipal Airport"

The bus bumped along the airport pavement grinding to a halt before the main terminal. Watching the numerous taxicabs, shuttle buses, and sport utility vehicles dropping passengers and their luggage at the lobby entrance, Anthony pointed out the window. Slapping her brother's arm, Catherine pressed her index finger against her lips.

"Shhh, we're supposed to be blind, remember?" whispered the perturbed girl.

"Your sister is absolutely correct," agreed Xerxes Xenon, floating toward the front of the expansive vehicle. "How do you know what is outside the window when you cannot see?"

"They can't see me looking. They're blind," whispered Anthony.

"The bus driver can see," hissed Catherine.

"He's..."

"Ladies and gentlemen, we have arrived at our destination," announced the driver, cutting short Anthony's rebuttal. "Thank you for using Charter Bus Lines. I hope you have a safe flight. Your escort is here to guide you to the terminal."

A tall woman stepped aboard the bus. A wind gust playfully tossed her long blond hair. She smiled at the bus driver and surveyed the passengers. Her eyes locked on the three children sitting on the rear bench.

"I didn't realize we had children on the tour with us. What a pleasant surprise. I know the kids in the hospital are happy to share their experiences with their peers. Why don't you three come to the front of the line," said the blond woman, moving toward the rear of the bus.

"Us?" stammered Anthony, sweat beading on his brow.

"Yes, you."

"That's not really necessary. We don't need to be at the front."

"Don't be silly. It's an honor, and it's about time we recognized the efforts of our youth," continued the woman, standing in the aisle.

"We don't deserve this," said Catherine, steadying her trembling hands. "We really, really don't deserve this."

"Modesty and humility are admirable qualities, and you portray those traits well. That makes it even more important that you represent the group."

"I didn't know we had kids, either," said a grizzled man with a long beard, sitting in the seat in front of Catherine.

"They probably just joined us for this trip," commented the man next to the bearded man. "No kid could travel as much as we do, especially attending school."

"True, you've got a point. Well then, we're glad to have you with us. The name's Billy, what's yours?"

"Uh...um...Catherine. And this is Anthony and Jeanne-Marie."

"Great to meet you. Hey, why don't you lead us into the airport?"

*Because we're not blind, and we're not flying to Colorado*, thought Catherine, rubbing her sweaty palms against her thighs. *I wish this guy wouldn't make such a big deal of having a few kids on the bus. No one was supposed to pay any attention to us. How are we going to get away from these people?*

"Sure," said Anthony, rising to his feet.

"That's the spirit, lad. We're right behind you. This is the kind of energy we need to start every trip," shouted Billy, clapping his hands.

The bus erupted in applause and gleeful shouts. Dragging their feet and smiling sheepishly, the three red-faced children meandered down the aisle. Clasping Catherine on the shoulder, the woman steered the little girl off the bus.

"Hold your sister's hand," instructed the woman, grabbing Catherine's right hand. "The airport is not busy tonight. We couldn't have planned this any better."

"We could have planned better," whispered Catherine, eyeing her brother.

"We're here, aren't we?" responded Anthony, his words drowned by the clamor arising from the excited group exiting the bus. "I'll handle this."

"This I've got to see," muttered Catherine, observing their smiling guide who appeared unaware of the children's fidgeting.

"Too bad you can't see. You're supposed to be blind, so just listen," said Anthony, clearing his throat.

"What are you going to do?" hissed Catherine, noting the distance they had put between themselves and the group unloading from the bus.

"Miss, there seems to be a slight mix-up here. We're not with the group. We're not even going to Colorado."

Catherine gasped and kicked her brother in the shin. Anthony winced, tears welling in the corners of his eyes. The lady stalled in her tracks and turned to face the three kids.

"What?" asked the woman, staring in disbelief.

"Yes, Ma'am, we were told to ride with the group because we need to meet our parents at the airport," continued

Anthony, rubbing his shin and glaring at his sister. "Billy's right. We've got school and can't make any tours. But..."

"That's quite understandable," said the woman, smiling softly. "I'll take you to your parents."

"They might not be here yet. But they told us to meet them in the lobby."

"No problem. The lobby is straight ahead."

Xerxes Xenon, who had been silently floating in front of the children, winked at Anthony. Catherine flashed a toothy, bashful grin and waved her hands apologetically. Limping, Anthony waved her off and snorted.

"Mommy's coming here?" asked Jeanne-Marie, confused by all that had transpired.

"Shhh...I don't know. We'll have to wait to see," responded Catherine, clamping her hand over her younger sister's mouth.

"What was that, Dear?" asked the woman, holding the door for Catherine and her brother and sister.

"Oh, nothing."

"Thank you, Ma'am. We'll wait over here," said Anthony, pointing to a row of green chairs.

"Okay, I'll see you in a minute after I help the others," said the woman, returning to the parking lot.

"Quickly, let's get out of here."

"No kidding," agreed Catherine. "Jeanne-Marie, you almost gave us away. But, don't worry. I was confused, too."

"What?" asked Jeanne-Marie, shrugging her shoulders.

"Never mind," said Xerxes Xenon. "There is an exit at terminal three. We must hurry. Our trip took longer than I anticipated, but it was no fault of yours."

Catherine gazed quizzically at Xerxes Xenon. *What's up with him?* thought the puzzled girl. *He never acts this nice.*

*Oh, well, it's better than his normal, sour attitude. I wonder how long this will last.*

"Over there," gasped Anthony, pointing to the rental car counter. "It's the police. Are they here for us? We can't let them see us yet, or they'll never believe our story. We don't even know where Richard and Jacqueline are hiding. I hope they're hiding and not trapped somewhere."

"Wait here," ordered Xerxes Xenon, darting toward the two officers.

"Catherine, get behind the snack machine. Those guys keep looking around like they're searching for somebody."

"That is because they are searching for somebody...three young children! A boy and his two little sisters," said Xerxes Xenon, appearing suddenly.

"Ah no, they got here too quickly. All because we had to ride that slow bus. If we could move as fast as the elements this would be no problem," muttered Anthony, leaning against the luminescent snack machine.

"For once, will you use your brain?" asked Xerxes Xenon, grimacing. "Brains win over brawn any day. You do not have to be physically superior to achieve greatness. We will outwit the police. Wait here, and I will distract them. When you see a green flash, run for terminal three. It will lead you onto the runway."

Anthony nodded. In a flash, Xerxes Xenon vanished. Catherine stared at the officers who fidgeted restlessly, continuously surveying the lobby.

The taller of the two officers shook his head and turned toward the children's hideout behind the vending machine. His partner's back was toward the kids. Resting his hand on the handle of the gun strapped to his side, the shorter officer frantically pointed behind the other officer. Spinning around, the policeman flung his hands before his face shielding his face from several green explosions. Both men sprinted toward the light.

"Now is our chance," said Anthony. Sweeping Jeanne-Marie piggyback style onto his back, he dashed into the terminal with Catherine close on his heels. A velveteen rope and a sign labeled "Men at Work" blocked their path. Without hesitation, Anthony stepped over the barrier and entered the tunnel.

"Over here!" shouted Xerxes Xenon, appearing before the fleeing group. "This is a jet-bridge where the airplanes connect to the building, allowing passengers to board the plane without having to leave the airport. Open this door. Hurry before the electricians return from their coffee break. We are fortunate they left this door unlocked."

"How do we get down?" asked Catherine, shoving open the door and peering at the ground far below her.

Squatting, Anthony waited for Jeanne-Marie to dismount from his back. Springing to his feet, he held his sister at bay and peered over the edge. Jeanne-Marie attempted to squirm her way closer to the end of the terminal.

"Jeanne-Marie, don't get too close!"

"Look, a ladder," said Anthony, pointing. "I'll go first, then Jeanne-Marie, and then you."

"Okay," answered Catherine, grabbing her younger sister's hand. "Don't look down."

The three children meticulously made their way down the ladder. Reaching the ground, they surveyed the large jets and baggage carts. Anthony and his sisters turned to Xerxes Xenon for directions.

"Hey, you kids, what are you doing out here?" yelled a man wearing blue overalls. "Officer, there are some kids loose on the tarmac."

"I see them. We'll get them. Kids, stop! It's the police."

"Run!" yelled Xerxes Xenon.

"Where?" asked Anthony, scooping Jeanne-Marie up again, piggyback style.

"For the first time in my life, I have no idea," admitted Xerxes Xenon. "Run for that large field. If Tabitha Tantalum and your brother and sister are out here, maybe they will spot us."

"Great," mumbled Anthony.

"Kids, stop," yelled the police officer, leaping a pile of suitcases.

"Run."

# "Ray's End"

"Where is Gary?" yelled Dr. James, ripping his glasses from his face and rubbing his eyes. "How long does it take to run a simple errand? Why can't I find good help these days? I'm surrounded by imbeciles!"

Jacqueline swallowed hard and buried her face in the crook of her arm. Lying with her abdomen against the warm earth, she, like her brother, attempted to conceal herself behind a plane's narrow tire. The aircraft's dark shadow added more protection. Yet Jacqueline did not feel secure listening to the men's boots crunching against the ground less than ten feet from her hideout.

The third member of the group, an average-sized man spitting sunflower seeds, spoke. "Evidently your man can't handle a bunch of little kids. Those kids are not my problem, nor were they part of the arrangement. You can take care of them on your own time. I'm firing up this baby, and we're taking off. You've got five minutes to make up your mind. Either you're on the plane, or you're not. It makes no difference to me. I get paid regardless."

"Lan, wait. How much do you want? If those runts get loose and rat us out, the authorities will be crawling all over this place. It will end your supply from this city," pleaded Dr. James.

"That is where you are wrong, Doctor. You provide only a small fraction of our business. Even though you have been dependable, we don't need you, especially if you jeopardize our operation by attracting the police. Take care of your kids your way. We don't get involved in domestic matters. If you become a liability, we will get rid of you."

Sweeping his straight, black hair under a baseball cap, Lan circled the plane. Spitting another few sunflower-seed shells on the ground, he climbed the steps to the cockpit. Pausing at the top of the steps, Lan glanced at his watch and eyed Dr. James before disappearing into the plane's cabin.

"This is what I get for dealing with a foreign crew," growled Dr. James. "I should have worked with that American group."

"But you know it's safer to work with these guys because it's harder to trace everything once it goes overseas," said Dr. Ray, running his fingers through his hair. "Forget about the kids, and let's deal with Lan. They're only harmless children. They shouldn't be involved in any of this. As adults, it's our responsibility to protect them."

"All of this sugary, sappy sentiment is making me sick again. Is that all you think about, saving and preserving the children? How safe do you think it is to have a bunch of brats running around spreading stories about our operation? It's too late. They're already involved. They must be silenced. It's easier to dump them over the Pacific Ocean than it is to bury them around here. But if Gary doesn't find his way back here, we'll have to do things the messy way. A set of young organs will fetch a lucrative price on the market."

"You are disgusting! Your soul is as black as tar. I won't have any part of murdering innocent children."

"Ray, you'll do as you're told. I don't want to hear another word from you. Finally, we have earned the right to meet our buyers face to face. I won't miss this opportunity. It could be worth millions of dollars of extra business a year. No whiny, runny-nosed urchin is preventing this from happening. Do you understand? Don't answer that. I know you don't understand, and it really doesn't matter. Because you have no say in this affair. Just keep in mind the debt you still owe me."

"Doctors, are you ready?" asked Lan, sticking his head out of the cockpit door.

"Yeah, here we come. Where is that dolt, Gary? Let's go, Ray. Those kids are now his problem."

"This is getting too dangerous," muttered Richard to himself. "I can't put my sister in harm's way. I have to think. What would the element's do? Come on, I'm a scout. I still have to do my good turn daily in order to follow the scout slogan. But this is going a little farther than what they meant by "Do a good turn daily." What am I talking about? Okay, I'm overanalyzing things. I have to relax. If I think about this too much, I'm bound to make a serious mistake. I just need to act and react."

Creeping on his elbows and knees, Richard inched toward Jacqueline. He saw that his sister had her head buried in the crook of her arm. Pausing, he glanced at the three men and then leaned toward Jacqueline.

"Jacqueline!" hissed Richard.

"What?"

"We have to distract them. Shoot some fireworks or something."

"What's that?"

"What? What's fireworks?"

"No, Goofy, that green light floating across the field."

"It's Xerxes Xenon," said Tabitha Tantalum. "Your brother and sisters must be with him. He wouldn't have come here alone. I'll guide them to us. Wait for me to return," ordered Tabitha Tantalum, disappearing.

"I can't get over how fast the elements move."

"The elements won't be able to move fast enough to stop those criminals. If we don't make a move, Dr. James will escape," whispered Richard, pushing his body into a crouch.

"Tabitha Tantalum told us to wait."

"We haven't come this far to let them get away. If you want to wait, that's your business. In the meantime, I'll distract them."

"Richard..."

Ignoring Jacqueline's plea, Richard turned his back on his sister. Sprinting from his concealed location, he raced toward the plane next to the one hiding his sister. Spotting the racing youth, Dr. James' eyes grew wide in disbelief. Drawing a revolver from under his coat and shoving Dr. Ray to the side, he aimed it at Richard.

"There they are!" crowed Dr. James, pulling the trigger repeatedly.

"No!" screamed Dr. Ray, leaping in front of Dr. James' weapon.

Richard dived to the ground. Turning his head, he saw Dr. Ray flinch and clutch his chest. The stunned doctor staggered and fell to his knees. He dropped to the ground and rolled onto his back staring into the sky.

"You idiot. If that's the way you want to go out, then you got it. I'm out of here. I have no intention of rotting in a dirty prison cell!" growled Dr. James, stepping away from his victim.

The plane's engine roared. With the propeller spinning at its maximum revolutions, the aircraft pitched forward. Dr. James spun about on his heels.

"Wait! Where are you going?"

"Police!" yelled Lan, leaning from the cockpit and pointing to the field.

Spotting three children pursued by several officers, Dr. James dashed after the plane. Flashing lights and wailing sirens flooded the end of the runway. The small aircraft rolled onto the runway leaving Dr. James clutching his side and waving his gun. He was out of breath from desperately chasing the plane.

"Dr. Ray, wake up!" screamed Jacqueline, crawling to the doctor's limp body.

"I hope..." choked Dr. Ray, coughing and wheezing. "...this will make up for some of the evil I've done in my life. Please forgive me."

"I forgive you. Don't die! You saved my brother's life."

"So that he can learn from my mistakes and do good where I did wrong." Releasing his breath in short spasms, Dr. Ray patted Jacqueline on the hand. "Don't worry about me. I feel so peaceful. Maybe I'll even see my dad. Leave me. I'll be okay. Go to your brother. He needs you." Squeezing Jacqueline's hand, Dr. Ray closed his eyes. The rise and fall of his chest ceased its labored effort.

"No, don't go."

"Dear child, it's okay. He has gone to a better place," said Tabitha Tantalum, stroking Jacqueline's cheek with the back of her hand. "Come with me. Your brother and sisters are here now."

"Anthony, stop the plane," yelled Xerxes Xenon, appearing on the tarmac with Jacqueline's siblings behind him.

"How?"

"Use your ring. Make a wall in front of the plane. Do it quickly before that winged flying machine lifts into the air."

Sliding onto his left knee and ignoring the approaching officers' shouts, Anthony pointed his ring at the aircraft. "By the power of the transition elements, I summon titanium!"

A silver-gray liquid metal flowed down the runway. Streaming under the plane, the titanium streaked ten yards in front of the aircraft. Surging upward, the liquid transformed into a shiny solid wall. With no time to stop, the plane plowed into the wall, crushing the front of the aircraft. The mangled propeller broke loose and spun along the pavement before imbedding itself in the ground. Both wings were wrecked and hung at odd angles. The titanium wall immediately vanished.

Stumbling from the cockpit, Lan swayed from side to side before crumpling into a heap on the concrete. Dr. James stood erect, having regained his breath after a short sprint down the runway. Facing a multitude of uniformed officers, the beleaguered doctor dropped his pistol. Racing past the children, three policemen apprehended Dr. James and secured him with handcuffs. A policewoman knelt over Dr. Ray's body and gently covered him with her coat. Bowing her head, she reverently stood beside the deceased.

Surveying the damage, a tall mustached man approached Anthony and his sisters. "Thomas, call the department and get the homicide division out here."

"Yes, sir," answered a short, stocky man sporting a goatee.

"This is unbelievable. What happened here?"

"More than he'll ever know," whispered Richard, joining his brother and sisters. "Great shot, Anthony!"

"Thanks. How are Ned Nitrogen and Caspar Calcium?"

"They're as healthy as ever," answered Tabitha Tantalum.

"Good, my heart can't take any more sorrow," whispered Jacqueline. "These adventures are taking a toll on me."

"Son, what's your name?" asked the officer.

"Uh, Richard."

"So, you're the one who left us the note at the hospital."

"Uh...a note?" asked Richard, rolling his eyes to his brother and sisters.

Anthony smiled nervously and tucked his head into his shoulder. Xerxes Xenon laughed and nodded. Catherine, holding Jeanne-Marie's hand, stepped forward.

"Excuse me, sir. This is a very long and confusing story. Maybe we should start at the beginning. We even know the location of another one of Dr. James' murder victims."

"I've got all night. Take your time," said the officer, flipping open a notepad and removing a pen from his shirt pocket. "What's the deal with wearing sunglasses at night? Oh, never mind, kids these days have new fashions every week. Let's hear about the matter at hand. I have a feeling this will be a long night. I'm all ears."

Clearing his throat, Richard winked at his sister. "It all began with a dangerous game of football..."

# Continue the Adventure!

Learn more about the characters, elements, and molecules through the following exciting books and game. Order yours today.

- Adventures of the Elements (the book that started the adventure)
- Rings of Enlightenment
- Dangerous Games
- Adventures of the Elements Scientific Trading Card Game

For information about new products including booster packs for the trading card game, the fourth book in the series, and other merchandise, visit the official Adventures of the Elements website. Also, you may purchase the books and game, join the club, or locate a retailer near you online. Visit our website for information about the National Adventures of the Elements Scientific Trading Card Game Tournament.

Industries or companies who wish to provide these educational materials to their local schools are welcome to contact us for detailed information. Teachers may become a school guardian and access a myriad of information through the website as well:
www.adventuresoftheelements.com

If you prefer traditional mail, you may reach us at:
Three Rivers Council #578, BSA
4650 Cardinal Dr.
Beaumont, TX 77705-2797

1-888-434-4140

Each book retails for..........................................$  5.95
Plus shipping and handling ..............................$  1.00/book

Each trading card game retails for..................$ 11.99
Plus shipping and handling ..............................$  5.95 for 1 to 5 games
                                                                           $  6.95 for 6 to 15 games
                                                                           $  7.95 for 16 to 25 games
Allow 4 to 5 weeks for delivery.

# Development of Adventures of the Elements:

**THREE RIVERS COUNCIL #578**
**Boy Scouts of America**

Adventures of the Elements (AoE) educational materials are developed in partnership with Author Richard James III and the Three Rivers Council, Boy Scouts of America. For nearly 100 years, Scouting has provided young people with exciting opportunities to acquire knowledge and learn values that will prepare them as future leaders and citizens.

These materials will inspire interest in chemistry while students have fun. Education through entertainment has been the cornerstone of Scouting. Parents and teachers can feel confident that Adventures of the Elements materials will not be commercialized but will remain true to its original purpose, education. AoE materials teach science and chemistry while reinforcing family values and do not include controversial material found in other similar contemporary products. There will be AoE materials available for the Cub Scouts Academic Program, chemistry merit badge, and Round-up incentive booster packs.

To locate a Scout Office near you go to: www.scouting.org and click on the site map and then the local council indicator.

Contact: Three Rivers Council #578, 4650 Cardinal Dr., Beaumont, TX 77705-2797

Toll free phone number: 1-888-434-4140

# What is Learning for Life?

Learning for Life is an educational program designed to meet the needs of youth and schools. It helps youth meet the challenge of growing up by teaching character and good decision-making skills and then linking those skills to the real world.

Developed by professional educators and child development experts, the age appropriate and grade-specific lesson plans of the Learning for Life program have been praised for their ability to get youth involved through the use of such teaching techniques as role playing, small group discussion, an reflective and dilemma exercises.

**VISIT LEARNING FOR LIFE ON THE WEB**

www.learning-for-life.org